MW00939265

PUCKED UP LOVE

LILI VALENTE

SELF TAUGHT NINJA

PUCKED UP LOVE

A Bad Motherpuckers Novel

By Lili Valente

Pucked Up Love © 2018 by Lili Valente

❀ Created with Vellum

Wanted: Discreet Dominant gentleman to teach maybe-submissive woman the rules of the game. No whips, chains, paddles, handcuffs, ropes, or toys. No nookie. No creepy stuff.
No butt stuff. No gluten.
Just the facts, Sir.
Serious inquiries only.
–CuriousCat4

When I see the ad in the Portland Alternative's "Love Wanted" section, I can't resist the urge to respond. Yes, it's dangerous—as a star forward for the Badgers I have a reputation to protect—but I miss the thrill of calling the shots in the bedroom and reading that ad is the first time I've laughed in months.

So I reach out to Curious Cat about the "educational" opportunity...

A few sizzling—and hysterical—emails later we arrange to meet. I'm hoping we'll have chemistry, and I might finally be on my way to getting over my ex-girlfriend.

And then the gate to the beer garden swings open and in walks Hailey.

My *ex* is Curious Cat, and this experiment just got a hell of a lot more complicated.

But I never back down from a challenge—on or off the ice.

I keep my educational offer on the table—six weeks of submissive lessons. Six weeks to learn how to drive a Dominant man crazy, and then we part ways as friends.

What do I have to lose? Except what's left of my heart?

Dedicated to Terri D. thanks for all you do!

CHAPTER 1

WILL

*E*verything I know about making love last I learned from my mom and dad,

My mother and father have an unbreakable bond that still inspires me every day. They are my heroes every bit as much as the hockey legends I've worshipped since I was a kid strapping on my first pair of skates.

The lessons they taught me about love are priceless, and are what made it so easy to give up my kinkier tendencies when the time came.

At least at first...

When I first met Hailey, she was an eighteen-year-old college kid interning for the summer with the Badger's physical therapist. With her perky blond ponytail, big blue eyes, and easy smile, she was innocence personified. She was also confident, driven, funny, and sexy in a subtle, unselfconscious way that drove me out of my damned mind.

I asked her out the day we met, even though the logical me insisted it was a dumb idea.

She was eight years younger than I was, inexperienced, sheltered—practically still a kid in a lot of ways. But she was also a cancer survivor, a fiercely self-assured young woman determined to do great things with her life, and her smile melted me from the inside out. I was helpless to resist her. She was beautiful in every sense of the word, and when we kissed for the first time, it felt so right I knew the moment she sighed and snuggled closer to my chest that I was never going to let her go.

I also realized that I was going to have to terminate my membership to the Playground, the secret BDSM club I'd been active in since my early twenties, and box up my handcuffs and paddle for the foreseeable future.

Maybe forever.

When we first got together, Hailey was a virgin and not a particularly experienced one, at that. I was the first man to undress her down to her bra and panties, the first to make her come, the first to taste her sweet, salty heat, and the first to push inside her, taking her virginity four months after our first date.

I'd never waited that long to take a woman to bed, but it was worth it. *She* was worth it. I would have waited years if that were what she'd needed to feel ready.

It was always making love with her. It was never just sex or fucking or getting off. It was a mingling of souls, a sacred communion, a way to worship at the temple of her beautiful body and even lovelier heart.

And for years, that was enough.

Love was enough.

I didn't think about the box of toys tucked away at the back of my closet. I unsubscribed from the Playground mailing list and averted my gaze when I drove past the places where our group used to meet to indulge our cravings for control or a lack thereof. I pretended that Will the Dominant was another person, an old friend who'd left on a long business trip, never to return.

My career was taking off at the same time, and the increased media attention made it relatively easy to keep that part of me peacefully dormant. As an up-and-coming star forward for the Portland Badgers, the last thing I needed was a sex scandal. I knew it wouldn't matter that I'd had the enthusiastic consent of every woman I'd tied up, spanked, or pushed down to kneel at my feet; the mere fact that I'd done any of those things would be a scandal.

So the Dominant inside me slept, while the rest of Will Saunders made a name for himself in the NHL and fell deeper and deeper in love with Hailey Marks.

And sure, sometimes I would wake up as hard as mid-winter ice, fresh from a dream featuring Hailey with her wrists bound behind her back, or Hailey draped over my lap, her ass red from the spanking she'd all but begged for with her defiance. But when that happened, I took care of it.

I jerked off in the shower or woke Hailey with my mouth between her legs, making her come so many times she didn't seem to notice that when I finally fucked her I rode her harder than I usually would. That I slammed into her with the force of a man who needed more than soft and sweet, who needed the sharper edges of love he'd checked at the door when he'd started dating an eighteen-year-old virgin.

I thought everything was fine—not perfect, but so much better than good.

Loving Hailey felt so right, so perfect, so meant-to-be that I never dreamt she would say no to the ring I'd offered her at the annual Badgers pre-season party. I was *that* certain that, by the end of the night, we would be celebrating our engagement with family and friends.

Instead her eyes filled with tears and she ran.

She literally *ran away* from me, jogging across the crowded rooftop dance floor and darting into a closing elevator before my brain could process that shit was not going as planned. By the time I made it down the fifteen flights of stairs, there was no sign of her in the lobby of the Nines Hotel or on the street outside.

Hailey makes her living as a personal trainer and self-defense teacher, so I wasn't surprised by her speed, simply shocked that she's used it to get away from me.

There had been no sign, no warning, not a single fucking clue that our relationship was on the rocks. We'd been making out in the limo on the way to the party, for God's sake, with her giggling and whispering for me to stop trying to slip a hand up her dress even as she wrapped her arms around my neck, holding on so tight I was sure she would never let me go.

But she did.

She not only let me go, she slammed the brakes on Us so fast it gave me whiplash.

When she finally answered my calls and texts three days later, she calmly explained that she still loved me, but that she had to say goodbye. She'd moved straight from her parents' house to the condo we shared and had never proven to herself that she was strong enough to survive on her own. She insisted she had to do that, had to prove she could make it without a parent or an older boyfriend looking out for her if she was ever going to feel like a whole and healthy person.

I tried everything I could to convince her that she didn't need to break up with me to feel complete—we could take a step back, live separately, or otherwise alter course without flushing our love down the toilet—but her mind was made up. And after five years together, I knew damned well that Hailey was every bit as stubborn as she is beautiful.

I knew fighting for her was a losing battle, but I fought anyway. I sent her gifts and letters and a shitty painting of a flower I made in the art class Wallace bullied me into taking with him in order to find a "healthy expression for my man pain."

But nothing I said, did, or gifted made a difference.

Finally, after the saddest six months of my life, I stopped calling, stopped texting, stopped driving by the gym we co-own in hopes of catching a glimpse of her through the window. I stopped being a pathetic, love-sick asshole and started back down the road to the man I was before, a man who knew how to control his body, his mind, his emotions, and the submissive woman in his bed.

I wasn't actively looking to get back into the scene, but the thought was definitely rolling around in my head, slowly becoming a temptation I didn't want to resist.

That's why I kept flipping the pages of the Portland Alternative free weekly until I reached the Love Wanted section, why I kept skimming until I reached the sub-seeking-Dom ads and came across a gem tucked away between several less imaginative offerings.

Wanted: Discreet Dominant gentleman to teach inexperienced,
maybe-submissive woman the rules of the game.
No whips, chains, paddles, handcuffs, ropes, or toys.
No sex.
No creepy stuff.
No butt stuff.
No gluten.
Just the facts, Sir.
Serious inquiries only.
−CuriousCat4

"But what if I can make you like the butt stuff, Curious Cat?" I murmur, a smile curving my lips as I flip open my laptop, create a new email account suitable for the occasion, and whip up a response to the ad.

To: CuriousCat4

From: GlutenFreeDiscreetGentleman

Subject: Maybe submissive?

Hello Curious Cat,

I saw your ad and was intrigued...

Why are you "maybe" submissive?

I could be interested in applying for the position of your Discreet Gentleman, but I don't have the time or patience for voyeurs. I do, however, have a significant amount of experience as a Dominant and a familiarity with the Portland scene that could prove useful if you decide you want to give any of the off-limits items on your list a whirl.

Several of them can be a lot of fun with the right person.

Care to tell me a bit more about where you're coming from?

And just FYI, I'm thirty-one, in top physical condition to meet the demands of my job, drug free, disease free, creepiness free, and I don't send people running in horror when they see my face, so you can be assured of an education from a well-kempt human being who flosses regularly. I also have three little sisters, a mother who means the world to me, a number of close female friends, and a healthy respect for women. You'll be safe learning the ropes with me, and I'm willing to meet in public for as long as it takes for you to feel comfortable taking things to a more private venue.

I'm sure it doesn't need to be said, but just in case—

please insist on a public meeting with whomever you choose to be your guide. There are a lot of shit-weasels out there in the D/s world, and I wouldn't want you to get hurt.

Sincerely,

Discreet G

P.S. I'm not actually gluten-free. If that was a real condition and not added for comic relief, we might have a problem. Bread and I are in a serious, long-term relationship.

I send the email and go about my life, not thinking of it again until I get home from my last beach weekend of the summer to find an intriguing response waiting in my inbox.

To: GlutenFreeDiscreetGentleman

From: CuriousCat4

Subject: More on my maybe...

Hello Discreet G,

Thank you so much for your lovely, gentlemanly response. It was appreciated, especially in light of the number of dick pics my ad inspired. I don't know why I didn't anticipate an influx of genitalia, but that's why I placed the ad in the first place—I realize I have a lot to learn.

So, more about me, and my maybe...

I can't go into too many specifics for confidentiality reasons—I don't like to kiss and tell—but the broad strokes are that I used to find the idea of being tied up or spanked by a lover disturbing and even a little scary. But now, after several months carefully considering the possibility of submitting to a Dominant man, I'm starting to find it...interesting.

But I repeat that I'm SERIOUS about the no sex or toys part of my ad. That wouldn't be part of our relationship. I'm just looking for someone who can explain the lifestyle in more detail and what would be expected of me as a submissive. I've done online research, but there's only so much a person can learn from a chat room.

And I confess I would like to meet a Dom in person to prove to myself that you're not all weirdos with unresolved mommy issues.

Sorry if that was offensive...

Like I said, I have no idea what I'm doing.

I'm probably crazy to even be considering this, but it's important to me to find out if I can make the submissive thing work. There's someone special I would like to be able to please in this way.

That's probably not a smart thing to say, either, is it? That I'm hung up on another man? But I want to be honest with you, Discreet. It sounds like honesty is a big part of the whole D/s thing.

And FYI, I'm twenty-three, also in excellent physical shape for my job, and attractive in a girl-next-door kind of way. Not that it should matter since our relationship will be purely platonic, but maybe knowing what I look like will put your mind at ease about meeting me in person, as well.

Thanks for reading,

CuriousCat4

P.S. The gluten-free thing was totally a joke. Bread and I are also in a long-term relationship. I run every morning so bread and I can be together at dinner every night ;).

To: CuriousCat4

From: GlutenFreeDiscreetGentleman

Subject: Bread lovers unite

Hello Cat,

Thank you for your honesty. It's appreciated, and you're right—honesty is vital in a D/s relationship in order to keep the experience safe, sane, and consensual, which is the goal of any Dom worthy of the title.

And I don't mind that you're hooked on someone else. I recently got out of a relationship myself, and I'm not looking for anything serious. That's not to say that if you enjoyed our training and changed your mind about getting tied up that I wouldn't oblige you, but I would absolutely make you beg for it first. ;)

Kidding! I'm kidding, I promise.

I get that you're SERIOUS about the platonic nature of this relationship, and I fully respect that.

I have to confess, however, that your commitment to bread is pretty sexy.

Hopefully this guy you're hooked on appreciates your loyal heart and the lengths to which you're willing to go to in order to please him.

Shall we discuss potential coursework before we meet?

Sincerely,

Discreet Gentleman

To: GlutenFreeDiscreetGentleman

From: CuriousCat4

Subject: Course Work

All right, Discreet, let's do this.

Lay it on me. What's the syllabus look like for something like this?

Anxious, but intrigued,

Curious Cat

P.S. If you get gross, I'm not going to respond. I just had to cut another potential Gentleman loose after he sent over erotic fiction featuring a lady robot sex toy with four breasts and two vaginas. *shudder*

To: CuriousCat4

From: GlutenFreeDiscreetGentleman

Subject: Zero sex robots

Dear Cat,

Glad you cut that other guy loose. Sounds like a nut job. Seriously, if you choose not to meet with me, you should probably find an alternative means of recruiting your submissive professor. Not to discourage your curiosity, but most of the men reading the Portland Alternative are ghoulish bottom feeders. I am the rare exception. ;)

Yours is the first ad I've ever responded to, if that gives my claim any street cred...

In any event, on to the potential syllabus:

Lesson One: Who's your Daddy? In this first segment of our course, we'll explore the many different flavors of Doms available for your submissive enjoyment. There are Master Doms who Top full time and expect 24/7 submission from their bottoms, Doms who keep the power exchange in the bedroom, Doms who like to be called Daddy and enjoy age play, Guide Doms who get off on helping their subs achieve personal and professional goals through the use of sexual discipline, Sadistic Doms who want to make you hurt and not always in the fun way, and a few fringe types who keep slave harems and shit that we probably won't need to go into in any depth.

That doesn't sound like what you're looking for with your special guy.

For my part, I'm a power exchange in the bedroom kind of Dominant. I like topping my girl when we're naked and keeping the power balance equitable the rest of the time. I enjoy a strong woman who knows her mind, and I honestly find it hotter to top someone like that than a person who spends her life as a slave to my every whim. I have a couple of friends who are really into the full-time Master gig, but I knew from the beginning that it wasn't for me.

If your special guy ends up being a 24/7 Master, you'll have to decide if you're up for that sort of situation. It's definitely a more intense commitment, though opening yourself up to being Dominated in the bedroom can be intense, too.

Which leads us to...

Lesson Two: Safe, sane, and consensual. We'll cover how to keep yourself emotionally, mentally, and physically safe, the use of safe words, and other etiquette you should know before you start playing around with power exchange.

Lesson Three: Exploring the nitty gritty of obedience to your Dom. We can start with some easy, non-sexual exercises that can be done in public if you don't feel comfortable meeting me in private at this point.

Lesson Four: Depending on how Lesson Three pans out, we can discuss punishments for disobedience and what some of those might be. We can also do some light role-playing to help you discover if you're the kind of submissive who enjoys being punished (most do) and how to balance obedience with your craving for punishment. (If this sounds crazy, don't stress. It will either make complete sense by the time we get to Lesson Four, or you'll have decided being a submissive isn't your bag and moved on to other things. No need to worry too much about this part right now.)

If all goes smoothly, we'll proceed onward from there until you feel ready to hop out of the nest, little sub, and go looking for the Big Bad Dom of your Dreams. Or the Daddy Dom of your dreams, or whatever Dom punches your particular buttons.

How does that sound?

It sounds like a blast to me. I'm looking forward to ushering you over to the dark side, Cat. I think you're going to love it here.

Sincerely,

Discreet

To: GlutenFreeDiscreetGentleman
From: CuriousCat4
Subject: I'm in.

All right. I'm in.

Let's set a time and place to meet before I chicken out.

How's Friday afternoon at six o'clock at the beer garden on Lombard? It's big enough we should be able to find a private table in a public setting.

Yikes, I'm nervous!! Please don't be weird in person, okay? You seem so nice via email. Please continue to be nice and don't show up looking like the crypt keeper or smelling like steamed broccoli or wearing a "I have the dick, so I'll make the rules" T-shirt. I saw a guy wearing one of those the other day, and it was all I could do not to dump my coffee all over his chest.

Sincerely and anxiously,

Cat

To: CuriousCat4

From: GlutenFreeDiscreetGentleman
Subject: See you Friday

Friday at six is perfect. I'll be coming straight from work and will have just showered, so I shouldn't look like a corpse or smell like steamed broccoli. And my mom raised me better than to buy a shirt like that, Curious, so no fear.

I'll be the guy wearing two watches on my left wrist. How will I know you?

To: GlutenFreeDiscreetGentleman
From: CuriousCat4
Subject: I'll be the girl with the...
...daisy in her ponytail.
Unless I chicken out.
Eep!

To: CuriousCat4
From: GlutenFreeDiscreetGentleman
Subject: Don't chicken out
I'm harmless, I promise. I also have a fairly recognizable face around Portland, so if you see someone familiar wearing those two watches, don't worry, it's me. And please, remember our mutual commitment to secrecy. I definitely need to keep our lessons on the down low for work reasons.

To: GlutenFreeDiscreetGentleman

From: CuriousCat4

Subject: Just between us

My discretion is assured, Discreet. This will be our secret, and I promise you won't regret taking the time to teach a newbie the ropes.

My sincere thanks,

Cat

For some reason—the guileless tone of her emails, perhaps—I believe her. I believe that Cat is who she says she is and that I won't regret the insane decision to meet up with a complete stranger for Dom lessons.

I believe it right up to the moment the beer garden gate swings open and Hailey walks through it, a white daisy tucked into her hair and an anxious expression on her pretty face.

My Hailey is Curious Cat, and this experiment just got a hell of a lot more complicated.

CHAPTER 2

Turn around. Leave! Run! Now! Before you get knocked out, dragged into a windowless van, driven across the border, and sold into human bondage somewhere in the dark heart of Honduras.

Ignoring the voice of panic, I tuck the daisy into my ponytail, square my shoulders, and push through the gate into the beer garden. It's a gorgeous early autumn afternoon in Portland, and throngs of beer-loving hipsters are already sidled up to the fifty-foot bar to my left, lounging at the picnic tables scattered throughout the open space, or tossing horseshoes with one hand while juggling a giant, salted, soft pretzel with the other.

There are far too many witnesses for there to be any risk of getting knocked out or dragged into Discreet Gentleman's van, and my gut says the man I've been emailing for weeks truly is the decent Dom he seems to be.

And if he's not, I've got a black belt in karate, ten

years of kickboxing experience, and four years as a self-defense teacher who drills disabling attackers bigger and stronger than I am on a daily basis. If D.G.'s looking for an easy mark, he picked the wrong Curious Cat.

Though, you know what curiosity did to the cat, right?

It killed it, Hailey.

Dead.

The curious cat is now a dead cat.

"Oh, shut up," I mutter, wishing the inner voice would give it a rest already. She hasn't been this chatty since I was an angsty twelve-year-old who grew six inches the summer before seventh grade and was certain everyone in my new middle school was talking about what a Sasquatch freak I was every time I slunk down the hall.

That was the last time I had the luxury of being a normal pre-teen with normal problems. Less than a year later, I was diagnosed with leukemia and swapped fighting to fit in for fighting for my life. Once I'd won that fight—two years and three rounds of chemo later—I'd learned not to sweat the small stuff.

And really, even though experimenting with sexual submission *sounds* kinky and a little scary, it's still decidedly in the "small stuff" category.

If I decide I don't like what I learn from Discreet Gentleman, then I can thank him for his time and walk away. That's it. No one dies or suffers from severe trauma or has to deal with chronic mental or emotional pain.

And then I'll finally know if I can be what Will needs me to be.

If the submissive shoe fits, I can go back to the man I love prepared to *truly* be the woman of his dreams. And if I can't, I'll be forced to admit that reconciliation is impossible, finish grieving the good thing I've lost, stop obsessing about my ex-boyfriend, and move on.

Of course, if the latter happens, it will be a death of sorts. My dreams of a life shared with my best friend will die. And my belief that love can conquer all—as long as you're willing to fight hard enough—will take a fatal beating.

But that's why I'm here tonight. To fight. To fight for Will and for myself and for the future I still, after nearly a year apart, can't imagine without him.

I amble around the perimeter of the garden, boots crunching in the pea gravel as I discreetly scan the crowd. There are a number of skinny college boys near the horseshoes working on adding a beer belly to their lanky frames, but none of them are wearing a watch— let alone two—and my Discreet Gentleman said that he was thirty-one. Though, of course, he could be lying. My sister Sabrina insists men live to pathologically lie on dating apps and via email—especially about things like age, being employed, and how much hair they've got left.

Discreet could be in his late thirties or even his forties for all I know.

I've never dated anyone that much older—I've never dated anyone but Will; a few low-key relationships my senior year of high school hardly count—but even if Discreet is older than he claimed, I'm not worried about the age difference. This isn't a *date*, after all. It's a meeting between a student and a professor. Yes, Discreet got a little flirty in his messages once or twice, but on the whole, he truly seemed to respect the fact that I'm on a hunt for knowledge, not experience.

If I decide I'm ready to experience any of the things I learn about, I only want to experience them with Will. He's the only man I've ever been with and the only one I *want* to be with.

But I have to be sure I can be what he needs.

I'll never forget the way he sounded the night I overheard him talking to that stranger in the slick gray suit, the one who looked far too refined to be drinking beer at a Portland Badger's season opener party...

"Are you sure marriage is the right choice, Will?" The man's voice is low, but his words carry to where I'm tucked into an alcove around the corner from where he and Will stand at the edge of the rooftop deck, looking out at the city. I'd sought shelter here when a cool breeze picked up a few minutes ago, and now I'm stuck—torn between the urge to reveal myself, and the temptation to eavesdrop on this unexpected conversation.

"She seems like a lovely girl," the man continues, "but you were never a dabbler. Dominance is part of who you are. I know you've taken a break from the scene, but are you really ready to make a permanent departure? To put that part of yourself on the shelf for good?"

"I love her, Sterling," Will says without hesitation, making my throat tight.

I love him, too. So much.

I've done a lot of things I'm proud of in my life—beating cancer, beating the devastating anxiety that came after, finishing college in three years, and starting my own business —but what I've built with Will is the thing that means the most to me. We work hard and play hard at this love, each of us committed to making our relationship more beautiful and sexy and fun with every passing day.

There is no doubt in my mind that we're meant to be, but I can't deny that the "Dominance" thing this Sterling person is talking about is coming out of left field for me. Since when is Will into that?

And what is that really? I mean, I saw the trailers for those kinky movies that came out a few years ago, but I was never curious enough to buy a ticket. I've never been intrigued by whips or chains or the idea of calling a man "sir" while we were naked. I'm way too self-sufficient for that.

"I know you do," Sterling says. "And she clearly adores you. But is it going to work until death do you part if you're not honest with her? If you deny something you need in order to feel complete?"

Will is quiet for a long moment.

I lean forward, ears straining as my pulse speeds faster.

"I don't know, but I..." He sighs, a weary, resigned sound that makes a sour taste fill my mouth. "But I can't go there with Hailey. She was a virgin when we got together, and she's completely inexperienced in anything but the most vanilla stuff in the bedroom."

My cheeks heat as irritation and embarrassment rush through my chest. I can't believe Will's talking about our sex life with a stranger!

Worse, I can't believe he considers our lovemaking "vanil-

la." I've always thought we had an amazing sex life—hot and heavy, but tender and connected at the same time. I've always treasured the time we spend in bed together and felt so lucky that my first lover was going to be my last.

Now, I feel like a naïve, ridiculous little girl—which I guess is what I deserve for eavesdropping. But now I'm trapped. I can't make a run for it without Will knowing that I was spying on him and realizing exactly why I'm upset.

"Then maybe you simply need to take the lead," Sterling says. "She might be more open to experimentation than you think."

My nose wrinkles and my jaw clenches as I fight the urge to tell this stranger to kindly stop talking about my sex life, but my anger fades as Will responds.

"No. She isn't submissive, Sterling. Not even a little bit. She's a sweetheart, but she's also a powerhouse, one of the toughest, most fearless people I've ever met. And I love that about her. I don't want her to change, so..." He trails off, and when he speaks again, he sounds so defeated it makes the backs of my eyes sting. "So I have to let the rest of it go, no matter how much I miss it sometimes."

My ribs lock down around my heart, and its all I can do not to burst into tears.

It's all a lie. My perfect love isn't so perfect, after all, and the man I adore above all else isn't happy in my bed.

A part of me insists that he didn't say he was unhappy—he said he had to let some things go—but the hurt swelling inside me is bigger than the voice of reason. The hurt and the shame hound me as I sneak back into the main part of the restaurant and rejoin the party. Their voices grow louder and louder as I force myself to smile and chat and dance with Will *to a slow song, then louder still as he pulls me back outside and drops down onto one knee.*

And even though his eyes are shining with love and hope, all I can see when I look into them is the reflection of a silly little girl who isn't enough for the man she loves so much it hurts.

I can't see the future anymore. I can't see that happy present I've taken for granted for so long.

All that's left is the lie and the knowledge of how much I've let Will down.

And so I run.

I run, and I keep running for a long, long time.

By the time I finally stop running from the pain—stop numbing it with too much exercise, too many long hours at work, too many late nights spent reading dark, dreary suspense novels until my eyes ache—it's been six months and Will has stopped calling and texting. He doesn't swing by the gym we co-own, he lets his financial advisor communicate the latest news on budgets and insurance for our business, and I realize that he's well and truly gone.

And that I'm well and truly not *over him.*

Not even a little bit.

And so I open up my laptop and type "Dominance and submission" into the search engine. Five months—and a crap load of reading later—I place my personal ad.

And now I'm here, scanning a bar for a man wearing two watches on his left arm, feeling increasingly anxious with every passing second.

And increasingly...scrutinized.

The skin at the back of my neck prickles, and the hair on my arms lifts. That place between my shoulders I can never quite reach begins to itch, and my fingers flutter anxiously at my sides. Someone is watching me —I can feel it. My Discreet Gentleman is here, concealed somewhere in the crowd.

No sooner has the thought zipped through my head than a deep, sexy voice behind me says, "Curious Cat, I presume?"

My throat locks, and my eyes go wide. That voice isn't just sexy as hell—it's also familiar. Insanely familiar.

But surely it can't be...

What are the odds?

A thousand to one?

A million?

But when I turn and look up at the man standing in the shadows at the end of the bar, where a metallic awning provides cover from the setting sun, I find Will's familiar hazel eyes staring down into mine, his familiar sandy-brown hair falling over his forehead on one side, his familiar lips curved in a sexy smirk, his familiar broad shoulders straining the fabric of his soft gray T-shirt.

My heart skips a beat, but before I can speak, he lifts his left arm—showcasing the two watches encircling his wrist, eliminating the last shred of doubt. "I'm sure this isn't what you expected. It isn't what I expected, either."

I swallow hard and nod, still too stunned to make a meaningful contribution to the conversation.

"I confess I'm not thrilled to learn that you're placing

personal ads in the Portland Alternative," he continues. "Especially not ads of this nature. I almost left when I saw the daisy in your hair. I was halfway across the parking lot to my truck when I turned around." He pauses, holding my gaze as he slides his hands into the pockets of his perfectly pressed black slacks. "Do you know why I turned around?"

I shake my head slightly, suffering from the worst case of cat-got-your-tongue-itis in recent memory.

Will steps closer, sending his spice, soap, and wood-smoke scent swirling through my head, making my mouth water. He must have come straight from prac-tice. His hair is still damp, his square jaw is shaven, and the clean smell of his skin summons a sharp curl of arousal low in my body.

All I want to do is lean into him, wrap my arms around his waist, and drag the tip of my tongue up his neck until his pulse beats faster. I want to nip his jaw with my teeth as he palms my bottom in his hands, squeezing my ass as he draws me close to where he's hard for me. I want him to pull me into the bathroom and take me against the wall—the way we did that summer in Vancouver when we were too early to check into our hotel room and couldn't wait two more hours to be naked and as close as two people can get.

But all of those things—things I once thought were sexy and a little wild—are child's play to Will.

The knowledge helps me stand my ground as he tips his face closer to mine and says in a husky voice, "Because if anyone is going to teach you about these things, it's going to be me. Not a creep you hook up with via a personal ad, and not some stranger who won't be satisfied with talk, no matter how many times he'll assure you he doesn't want you down on your knees ready to suck his cock."

I pull in a sharp breath, but when Will leans even closer—so close his lips brush my ear when he speaks again—I stand my ground.

"So I will teach you what you want to know," he continues softly, "help you decide if you want to submit to this new man in your life, on one condition. You don't speak his name, you don't mention what he does for a living, you don't do anything that might make it possible for me to figure out this dickweed's identity. Because if I find out who he is, I will be tempted to beat the shit out of him, Hailey, and I know you don't support unprovoked physical violence."

Pressing my lips together, I close my eyes for a moment, fighting to think clearly through the arousal buzzing through my veins. There is no other man— there's only Will, there will only ever be Will—but I can't tell *him* that. Not now, not until I know for sure that I can be that girl, the one ready to get down on her knees for him and enjoy submitting to her man.

This has to be as authentic for me as it is for him or it's never going to work. And until I know for sure, I have to stand behind the shield of my lie, for both our sakes.

So I simply nod my agreement, though I can't resist asking the question that's been plaguing me since that overheard conversation last September, "Why didn't you tell me? About this part of you?"

He sighs, and some of the tension eases from his broad shoulders. "Good question. But it's not really relevant now, is it?"

Yes, it is, Will. It's completely relevant because I'm doing this for you. I want to be what you *need me to be, and I could have tried so much sooner if you'd only been honest with me.*

But I can't say those things, so I give a noncommittal roll of my shoulder. "I guess not."

"First lesson tomorrow night," he says, his voice harder than it was before. "I'll come over to your place after the game. Somewhere between eight and ten o'clock, depending on overtime."

"All right, sounds good," I say, but it doesn't sound good. It sounds terrifying and dangerous and like something that could get out of control very quickly.

"See you then, Curious." He leans in, pressing a whisper-soft kiss to my forehead that sends a wave of longing rushing through me, so sharp and sudden it nearly brings me to my knees.

I remain upright, but it takes all my strength to keep my legs steady and my face from crumpling as Will steps back, salutes me with his two-watch arm, and turns to walk away.

The man I love is back in my life so much sooner than I expected.

I'm not ready, not even close, but I've learned that the universe doesn't always wait until you're ready to send the next obstacle crashing through your door. I've also learned that obstacles aren't always bad things. Sometimes they're necessary challenges, mountains you have to climb in order to prove to yourself that you're ready to tackle anything that stands in your way.

As I sidle up to the bar and order a Grapefruit Hefeweizen to calm my nerves, I send out a silent prayer that I'm up to the challenge of Lesson One and everything that might come after.

CHAPTER 3

**From the texts messages of Hailey Marks
and Sabrina Marks**

Hailey: Hey, are you still at work or can you talk?

Sabrina: Still at work, so I can't talk, but I can text.
Happy hour is super slow so far. I told Brian not to cut
the bar snack budget, but he never listens to me. Now
we're losing hundreds of dollars in drink sales so he can
save ten dollars on hot dogs and buns. Ugh! What a
moron! I can't wait until he gets fired and Mona is
promoted to manager. Speaking of hot dogs, how did
your meeting with Discreet go?!
You chickened out right? Because there's no way in hell
you're stupid enough to go meet some Dom weirdo you
picked up with a personal ad. This was all a prank to see

how far I'm willing to take my newly embraced wild-girl side, right, big sis?

Hailey: Um…no. It wasn't.
And if you thought I was being stupid, you should have told me! I respect your opinion and want you to tell me if you think I'm doing something crazy!

Sabrina: No you don't. You're the most stubborn person I've ever met, Hailey Rae. Once you've made up your mind, you're going to do what you damn well please, no matter what I, Mom or Dad, the Pope, the Dalai Lama, or anyone else has to say about it. I learned that a long time ago, girl, and vowed to quit flapping my lips in vain.
But now you have me worried…
So, you actually went to meet this guy?!
Are you okay?
Was he awful?
What am I saying? Of course he was awful. He's a creepy personal-ad-answering Dom douchebag.
Ugh! If he hurt you, I will rip off his arms and beat him with the bloody stumps. Though, you probably already did that, didn't you? Since you're the queen of self-defense? I have to confess that your ass-kicking skills are part of the reason I wasn't too worried about this bonkers plan of yours. I figured if any creep tried some-thing with you, he'd be limping home with all his fingers broken and his balls wedged in his lower intestine.

Hailey: I have never broken anyone's fingers, and Discreet wasn't a creep.
He was something worse...

Sabrina: What's worse than a creep? A zombie? A clown? A dude who enjoys dressing like a baby and having his adult diaper changed?

Hailey: Ew! How do you even know about this stuff?

Sabrina: I read widely in the kinky-books section, sister dear. You should try it some time. Maybe then you would be satisfied reading about kinkery like the rest of us and not feel compelled to try out naughty stuff in real life.

Hailey: You know why I feel compelled to try it out in real life. You're the only person who knows. That's why I'm texting you instead of one of my other friends, who would give me less shit for being experimental.

Sabrina: Yes. I know. And I know you miss Will and are still madly in love with him and want to make it work, but... I don't know, Hails. Maybe you misunderstood what you overheard that night at the party or took it out of context or something. Will certainly didn't seem like he was unhappy or stifled or whatever in your relationship. He wasn't unhappy until you ended it and broke his heart.

Hailey: I didn't misunderstand what I heard, Bree. Will

was denying a vital part of himself in order to be with
an uptight good girl who had only slept with one guy in
her entire life.

I know that for a fact.

And you know how I know?

Guess who was waiting for me at the beer garden,
wearing the sexy black slacks I bought him for
Christmas three years ago and two watches on his
left wrist?

Sabrina: OMG no! No way!

Hailey: Yes, way. Will is Discreet! Discreet is Will!
He's so eager to get back to his old life that he's trolling
personal ads! And he was totally flirting with Curious
Cat. I've been rereading our emails for over an hour,
and it's there, simmering between every line. I can't
believe I didn't see it sooner. And now I want to punch
him in the teeth for flirting with someone online, even
though we broke up almost a year ago.

Sabrina: But he was flirting with YOU, Hailey.

Hailey: But he didn't know it was me!

Sabrina: Okay, okay, but he knows it's you now, right?
So how did that go? Did you tell him he was the reason
you were looking for a Discreet Gentleman in the first
place? Because you want to please him in all ways and
be his perfect little foot-licking fiancée, after all?

Hailey: I do not want to lick his, or anyone else's, feet. Power exchange in the bedroom isn't always—or even often—about performing humiliating tasks. It's a lot more layered and interesting than that. And no, I didn't tell him, because if I tell him and I turn out not to like the submission stuff after all, he'll be hurt all over again. And I can't stand to do that to him.

Sabrina: I imagine he's pretty hurt that you're out looking for a guy to Dominate you, too, right? I mean, especially since he was evidently concealing that part of himself from you for all the years you were together because he thought you wouldn't like it.

Hailey: Actually... No, he didn't seem hurt.
He was a little miffed at first, and said he almost walked out of the bar without letting me know he was Discreet, but then he shrugged it off and...

Sabrina: And what?! Don't keep me in suspense!

Hailey: He said...
He said he was still up for giving me lessons.

Sabrina: Ha! Well, of course he is. He wants back in your pants like a hermit crab wants a new shell, baby.

Hailey: How is Sheldon? I'm so proud of you for keeping another living thing alive for over three months.

Sabrina: Sheldon is fantastic and enjoying the larger aquarium I scored at a yard sale last weekend, but we're not changing subjects, psycho.
What did you say to Will?! Are you letting him back into your pants? I mean, I get that he is allegedly a complete sex god in the sack, but don't you think that will be painful for both of you if this experiment doesn't end well?

Hailey: I told you from the beginning, Bree, these lessons aren't about sex. They are sex-free, toy-free, butt-stuff-free lessons. Platonic lessons.

Sabrina: And I'm the queen of France.

Hailey: France doesn't have a queen. Not since they chopped the last one's head off.

Sabrina: And you've had your head chopped off if you believe Will doesn't want more than platonic teaching time with you. If you do this, things are going to get sexy, Hailey.

Hailey: For someone who's never had any, you have a lot of strong opinions about sex, Sabrina.

Sabrina: Yeah, well...I do a lot of reading. And thanks for the reminder that I'm a freakishly old virgin who's never going to get laid.

Hailey: I didn't mean it that way. I'm sorry. You could

get laid any day of the week, and you know it! You're so beautiful and smart and funny. But I respect you for waiting for that perfect guy who is man enough to deserve you. You've got a good head on your shoulders, little sis.

Sabrina: Blah. Whatever. I'm just picky.
And seeing how well Will treated you has made me impatient with assholes who only want to stare at my tits and talk about themselves. A guy hit on me at the beer festival last weekend. He asked my name—that's it. After that, it was a thirty-minute lecture on all the reasons he was awesome. He couldn't have cared less what I thought, felt, did for a living, liked or disliked— zero, zilch, nada.
He saw blond hair and big boobs and that was all he needed to know.
I could have been a blow-up doll for all he noticed my personality.

Hailey: I'm sorry, babes. Men in their early twenties are awful. I always felt lucky that I got to bypass them and go straight to someone more experienced.

Sabrina: You were lucky. And you still are. Will clearly isn't any more over you than you are over him. You guys can still totally make it work.

Hailey: Did you miss the part where he was offering to be a sex tutor to some strange girl he met via a personal ad?

Sabrina: A platonic sex tutor. You made that very clear. And he wouldn't have let the offer stand once he knew you were Curious Cat if he didn't want to get back together.

Hailey: I'm not sure about that. He was so cool... Detached in a way I've never seen him before.

Sabrina: Maybe that's his Dom side... Was it hot?

Hailey: Um...yes. It was.

Sabrina: Lol!
Well, then it sounds like you guys are off to a good start.
Talk to him, Hailey.
Clear the air and move forward as a team.
You two were always an incredible team.

Hailey: I'll think about it. We're meeting tomorrow night for Lesson One. So if you think I'm crazy, speak now or forever hold your peace.

Sabrina: I think you're crazy, but I also think you should go for it.
But I would like to be spared the gory details if that's all right. I enjoy reading kinky fiction, but hearing about the kinky shit you're getting up to with my future brother-in-law might make things weird at family holiday celebrations.

Hailey: It might not work, Bree. There's an excellent chance that we're not going to get back together.

Sabrina: And there's an excellent chance hot dogs are going to come flying out of my ears. I wish they would actually. If I had hot dogs, I could put them on the warming coils near the door so the sweet odor of meat would waft out into the street and lure in customers. If I don't get someone in here drinking soon, I'm never going to make rent by the fifteenth.

Hailey: You could always go back to modeling part-time. It wouldn't have to be forever. Just until you get enough money saved up to go back to school.

Sabrina: No. I'm done with that. I'm a serious woman, and I'm going to study serious things like abnormal psychology. I'm also going to make some seriously strong drinks so my patrons will keep coming back for more even without hot dogs to sweeten the happy hour pot. I've got this.

Hailey: Of course you do. No doubt in my mind. But if you need money to help cover rent, don't hesitate to ask. Business is good at the gym, and I just got hired to teach my teen self-defense course at the middle and junior high schools in the district. I start next week, and I'll be rotating through twenty-five schools before the end of the year. And if all goes well, the powers that be want to make it an ongoing thing.

Sabrina: That's amazing, sissy! I'm so proud of you. I get so psyched when I think about these girls being able to defend themselves and their friends from assholes if they need to. It gives me hope.

Hailey: Me, too. But I never could have done it without Will...

Sabrina: Not true. You could have gotten the start-up money for the gym somewhere else. You had a killer business plan.

Hailey: I'm not talking about the start-up money. I'm talking about support, encouragement, partnership, the man I love...
That's what I'm most afraid of, Bree.
What if Will's not the person I thought he was? What if I start down this road with him and at the end of it, the man I thought I knew isn't there anymore? What if I end up with a stranger?
I swear...
I would almost rather lose him and keep the man I think I know alive in my memories than learn that the Will I loved was never real to begin with.
Is that crazy?

Sabrina: No, it's not crazy. It's a little bit of a mind-bender, but I think I get it.
But it's like you always tell me—it's okay to go out alone after dark as long as you're prepared.

Hailey: I do say that, but you've lost me...

Sabrina: Yes, the world is scary. Yes, the streets are more dangerous for a woman alone than for a man. But if we take safety precautions, educate ourselves, and have a plan to deal with any threats, there's no reason a woman can't walk alone after dark. We deserve the same freedoms that men enjoy, and it's worth a little risk not to live in a fear-shadow all the time. Right?

Hailey: Right. No fear-shadow. I just have to trust my gut, and my gut says that Will is still the man I fell in love with five years ago. But he's also someone else, too. And I want to know that someone. If we're going to promise our lives to each other, I want all of him, not just the parts he's decided are acceptable for innocent Hailey's fragile eyeballs. I'm not eighteen years old anymore, and I have a few fantasies I've never told him about, too. He has no idea what I can or can't handle. I'm a lot tougher and braver and more experimental than he thinks I am.

Sabrina: That's the spirit! Show him what you're made of, baby. Though, judging by your badass levels, I think you might be better off Domming than subbing.

Hailey: It takes as much discipline and strength to submit as to Dominate, Bree. In a functional D/s relationship, the sub is every bit as strong as his or her Dom —at least mentally.

Sabrina: Well, well... Sounds like someone's done her homework. Then go get your spanking or whatever, lady, but keep the details close to your chest. I'm all about supporting your girl power, but I'd also like to be able to look Will in the eye without blushing bright red.

Hailey: Of course. I won't kiss and tell, I promise.

Sabrina: So you admit there's going to be kissing! Ha!

Hailey: Oh shut up and go buy some hot dogs. Tell Brian the cost is coming out of petty cash and you don't want to hear another word about it unless he likes looking at a line of empty bar stools.

Sabrina: Yes, ma'am. Off to explore my Dominant side right now. And good luck. Seriously. I hope you and Will work it out, whatever weird way that needs to happen. You two were so good together. I hated to see it end.

Hailey: Me, too, babes.
Me too...

CHAPTER 4

WILL

*A*fter nearly a decade as a Portland Badger, I don't get worked up over pre-season games anymore—I know my job is secure and management wants to keep me around—but I'm especially cool and collected tonight.

By the third period, I've slammed two pucks past the Red Wing's goalie and been on the ice longer than any other player except Wallace, whose endurance is being challenged while our other goalie recovers from a testy groin.

Wallace is also testy, but his irritability is coming from his brain, not his groin. The kid lets the stress get to him sometimes. I talked him down from the edge during the second intermission, but now, with five minutes still left on the clock in the third, he looks rattled in the cage.

"You've got this, Walls," I shout as I circle around the back of the net, getting ready for the faceoff after a close call with the Red Wing offense and a lucky save involving Wallace's skate blade.

"And we've got you." Petrov, our biggest, baddest defender slaps Wallace on the shoulder on his way by. "No more blown coverage. We're keeping it on their end of the ice for the rest of the night."

Petrov is a man of his word, and a player I'd trust with my life, let alone my team's defense, but a man's word is only as strong as his stick. When Petrov's shatters mid-slap-shot seconds after they drop the puck, we're right back where we started, scrambling to give Wallace cover as the Red Wing offense pushes in hard and fast.

A single breath is all it takes for my laser-focused brain to calculate the distance between myself and the net and realize there's no way I'm getting in position to offer cover in time. Thinking fast, I shout, "Petrov, over here!" The moment he makes eye contact, I toss my stick his way. He catches it in one meaty fist, lunges forward—sliding in between our net and the Detroit winger—and intercepts the puck, knocking it up the boards.

Launching into motion, I chase, empty-handed, after the puck. But I don't need a stick to kick the shit out of that biscuit. My skate connects with the spinning disc, sending it skidding harmlessly to center ice. The next line jumps over the boards, and I cruise back to the bench, where Petrov is already waiting with my stick and a clap on the back and Coach jokes, "You've got a future in the soccer major leagues after you retire,

Saunders. One hell of hustle. That's the way it's done, kids. Learn from your elders."

"That means you're old now, too, Saunders," Brendan, our captain, calls out from the other end of the bench. "Welcome to the club."

Laughter ripples through the rest of the team as I smile and shoot a stream of water Brendan's way. Four shifts later, the Red Wings are still scoreless and I'm on my way down the tunnel, feeling good about life.

Yes, things with Hailey and I are in a weird, fucked up place.

Yes, I want to kill this guy she's so eager to get on her knees for—hunt him down, turn him inside out, and slowly pull his face through his asshole—but I'm a Dominant man in control of my emotions and behavior who just played one hell of a good game. Besides, no matter how hard Hailey is crushing on this mystery douchebag, at least for tonight, she's mine.

Mine all mine, and I can't wait to get my curious girl alone and give her a preview of the things a real Dom can make her feel.

Careful, man. She's sub-curious, not sub-committed. Charge in there with alpha guns blazing, and you're going to scare her away.

My jaw clenches at the thought. A part of me thinks it's a decent strategy—if she's scared of the lifestyle, then she won't end up in bed with some piece of shit motherfucker who isn't me. The other part of me, the more optimistic, hopelessly romantic part, believes that as soon as Hailey's had a taste of what I can give her, she

43

won't want to go looking for her sub-high anywhere else.

She still loves me—I could see it in her every gesture, hear it whispering between every word she spoke. She loves me, but she wants to see what else is out there. I can empathize, but I'm also perfectly capable of giving her the variety, spice, and danger she's craving. She can have her cake and eat it, too.

And if I play my cards right...so can I.

I never imagined Hailey had any secret submissive fantasies. She's such a strong, fearless, badass woman— it's one of the things I love best about her. But that fiercely independent streak would also make it erotic as hell to top her. She's not the kind to submit easily—I'm going to have to earn every scrap of obedience, but it will be worth it.

Worth it, and so fucking hot I'm already sporting a semi on the way up the stairs to Hailey's new apartment.

The thought of Hailey on her knees in front of me, wearing nothing but a pair of lace panties, with her delicate wrists bound in rope and her eyes cast down because I told her to keep her gaze fixed on the floor until I give her permission to look up, drives me crazy. I want that from her—*with* her. I want it so badly I have to pause on the landing of her hallway, taking a moment to banish all erotic thoughts from my mind.

I have to maintain control or I'm going to give myself away five minutes into Lesson One. Hailey wants platonic advice from a friend, and that's exactly what I'm going to give her.

At least until she begs me to give her something more...

Outside her door, I knock softly, willing my pulse to remain steady as I hear her footsteps padding across the floor. I will not lose control, I will not let her see how desperate I am to have her back in my arms, in my life, in my bed.

I'm feeling relatively steady until she opens the door wearing nothing but a pair of glossy, skintight black leggings and a gray tank top with no bra—no bra for fuck's sake, *fuck me*, no fucking bra—and my blood pressure skyrockets.

CHAPTER 5

WILL

"*Hi*." Hailey's eyes widen as her gaze flicks up and down, taking in my freshly shined Ferragamo loafers, dark gray suit pants, and perfectly pressed white button-down. "I thought you said we were staying in?"

"We are, but I believe in dressing appropriately for a professional situation." I step inside, chest aching as I catch the familiar vanilla, flowers, vegetable stir-fry, and sunshine smell of a space where Hailey makes her home.

This smell is home to me, too—*she's* home to me—but I'm not the Will she lived with for five years. I'm William Major Saunders, Dominant Professor at large, and I refuse to let my pupil off the hook for sloppy presentation simply because the sight of her in sexy leggings and free-range breasts makes me want to cuddle her on my lap and fuck the hell out of her in equal measure.

"Oh, well..." Hailey closes the door behind me, clearly sensing my displeasure. "So do you want me to go change, or..."

I turn back to her, dragging my gaze away from the reclaimed wood dining table, bright blue couch, and pale pink chairs in her combination living room-dining room. The unfamiliar furniture is a physical reminder of how far she's moved on from the life we shared, and it pisses me off to a ridiculous degree.

And it makes me sad, but none of that shit is on the emotional menu tonight.

Not mad or sad, just strong, calm, and controlled. So I force a light note into my tone as I reply, "Yes, I would like you to go change."

Hailey's lips quirk uncertainly on one side. "You're serious?"

"I'm serious. Go change. And put on a bra, please."

She huffs as her cheeks go pink, the soft sound expressing an eloquent mixture of irritation, embarrassment, and amusement. "All right, William, I will. But *you're* the one who said we were just talking tonight. You'll have to forgive me for assuming I didn't need to be dressed to the nines to sit on my couch and take notes."

I step closer, and she backs away a matching step, her shoulders hitting the wall behind her.

Slowly, deliberately, I place my palms flat on either side of her face, leaning down until only a few inches separate my lips from hers. "First submissive lesson— when the Discreet Gentleman who's agreed to advise you asks you to go get dressed and put on a bra, you say 'yes, sir' and do as your told. Otherwise, the Discreet Gentleman is going to assume you would like to be punished for disobeying a direct order."

Hailey's eyes widen, awareness flickering in those deep blue depths even as her nostrils flare in that "You've Pissed Me Off" way I know so well. "We're just talking tonight, not playing or having a scene or whatever you call it. I haven't agreed to any rules or picked a safe word or done any of the things you're supposed to do before punishments enter the picture. I've done my homework, Will. I know how this is supposed to work. At least enough to know that right now you're being a dick, not a gentleman."

I grin, I can't help it—I've always loved Hailey's fiery side. "You have a point, Curious Cat. But you're the one who started playing games, sweetheart. I was just following your lead."

She lifts her stubborn little chin. "I have no idea what you're talking about."

I angle my head closer to hers until I can feel her body heat warm on my face. "You knew I was coming over. You knew that we would be alone in your apartment, and you chose to wear a semi-sheer shirt and no bra. Why would you make that choice, Hailey? What were you trying to prove? What consequences did you want to face?"

"I…" She swallows. "I don't know."

I tut softly. "That's not going to work. Honesty is mandatory during these lessons. I need you to be honest

49

with me, and even more importantly, I need you to be honest with yourself."

"I am being honest," she whispers. "I guess I just... wasn't thinking."

I hum as I draw back far enough to cast a pointed glance down at the front of her shirt, where her nipples are pulled tight, poking temptingly against the well-worn T-shirt fabric, the sight of them making me ache. "So you weren't thinking about making me suffer? About flaunting the beautiful body you've made it clear you no longer want me to touch?"

She shakes her head, and when she speaks, it's in a voice I can tell comes straight from her heart. "No, Will. I swear I wasn't doing that. I would never do that. I... I care about you. So much. I don't ever want to hurt you. Not ever again."

I nod slowly but keep my focus on those tight, tempting nipples. "So should I assume you chose to skip the bra because you secretly want to cross the platonic line you've drawn in the sand?" I drop one hand to her waist, teasing my fingers beneath the hem of her kitten-soft shirt, loving the way her breath catches as my fingertips graze her warm skin. "Because I would love to teach you to submit the fun way. Chatting and study can be informative, but you're not going to learn to ride unless you get on the horse."

Her breasts rise and fall, and the tip of my tongue begins to tingle.

Fuck, I want her nipples in my mouth.

Now. Five minutes ago.

We shouldn't rush into power exchange—the rules

are important and shouldn't be taken lightly—but I want her naked and under me so badly it's almost impossible to keep from lifting her into my arms and making a break for her bedroom.

It's been nearly a year since I've been with a woman. There's been no one since Hailey. I've had more than my fair share of opportunities—Puck Bunnies wait by the exit at every away game, and a good number are usually wearing my number, a sign they're eager to come back to my hotel room and puck me all night long.

But no matter how lonely and sexually frustrated I've been, the thought of a one-night stand or, God forbid, starting a relationship with another woman makes me sick to my stomach.

I don't want another woman. I want this woman, this sweet, sexy, delicious woman. I want her tits in my mouth, her pussy hot and tight around my dick, her voice in my ear as she calls out my name, begging me to make her come, to make her mine again.

And now, thanks to our emails, I also want her arms and legs bound to the four corners of her bed. I want to watch her muscles flex as I tease her nipples, licking and sucking and biting ever so gently until she's panting for more. I want to torment her until she demands I end her suffering, until she bucks and thrashes beneath me, waging a futile war for her freedom. But the bonds will be too tight, too expertly wrought for her to escape using brute force.

She'll have to learn to submit, to beg, to thank her master for her pain and her pleasure. And when she's put herself fully into my hands, I'll teach her the dance of suffering and satisfaction, take her to the edge of pleasure/pain where I'll make her come so hard she'll be ruined for vanilla sex for good.

The thought is so tempting that my cock swells thicker, harder, until it feels like my heart is beating in my heavy, suffering balls and every nerve in my body is humming with need.

"So what do you say, sweetheart?" I let my palm glide beneath her shirt, molding to her ribs. "Do you want to learn the boring way? Or do you want me to make you so wet you'll be soaked through these sexy little pants before we're halfway through our first lesson?"

She lets out a soft moan, and her lashes flutter. Her back arches, bringing her diamond-hard nipples even closer to my chest—a silent plea for me to give them the attention they so clearly crave.

But instead of falling into my arms with her mouth crashing into mine, Hailey darts to the right, her hands clutching her T-shirt just above her belly.

"I'm sorry, I don't feel well," she says, shaking her head. "I think I ate something. Something bad."

I blink, but before I can switch gears and ask if she's all right, she turns and makes a break for the back of the apartment.

"Gotta go," she calls over her shoulder as she jogs away. "Bathroom emergency. Can't be stopped. You should go; we can reschedule for another night." A moment later, she dives into a room halfway down the short hallway and slams the door behind her, locking it with a finality that makes it clear our erotic evening is over before it can begin.

I cross my arms over my chest, eyes narrowing as I study the light streaming from beneath the bathroom door, smelling a rat in this sudden "bathroom emergency." I stalk slowly forward, crossing the ultra-feminine space Hailey's created—silently thinking that I would have been fine with her transforming our apartment into a pink and powder blue, flower-packed hideaway if that's what she needed to exert her identity—until I reach the closed door.

"Are you all right?" I ask. "Can I get you anything? Medicine or some hot tea?"

"No, thank you, you should just go," she says, voice strained. "Please. I don't want you to hear this. It's going to be embarrassing. I think I ate eggs by accident or something. Probably that ice cream my sister brought over that I had for dessert tonight. I think it was custard." A frustrated huff is followed by a moan that doesn't sound sufficiently tormented to be believable. "God, I can't believe I forgot that custard has eggs in it. What was I thinking?"

"Don't blame yourself." I lean in, ears straining, but the only sound from within is the buzz of the fan whirring in the silence. "Ice cream shouldn't have eggs in it. That's clearly a violation of logic and decency."

She laughs softly, thinly. "Yeah, but seriously, Will, I need privacy. I'm going to be fine, I just need you to go. Now. Please."

"All right." I step back with a sigh, realizing I have no choice but to admit defeat. Whether Hailey's truly ill or hiding from the way the thought of playing sex games with me made her feel, I've got no choice but to retreat, regroup, and return to fight another day.

But I will be back.

I'm not giving up on her—or us—this easily.

"Feel better," I say. "I'll text you to set up a make-up session for Lesson One."

"Okay. Bye. Thanks. Bye!" Hailey squeaks, clearly ready to be rid of me.

With one final hard look at the locked door she's placed between us, I turn and walk away, locking her front door behind me to ensure she's safe. I take the stairs to the ground floor and elect to walk home instead of calling a car, hoping the exercise will help banish the frustration from my bloodstream.

But by the time I reach my condo complex ten blocks away, I'm still itching in places that can't be scratched, and my jaw is locked so tight I'm afraid I'll crack a molar if I try to go to sleep in my present state.

So I pour myself a generous tumbler of bourbon and sip it as I start the shower, turning the taps until the water is steaming hot. I just showered less than an hour ago—I always grab one the second I get off the ice—but that was a utilitarian shower.

This is a therapeutic one.

As I step into the steam, I set my glass on the end of the tile bench and turn my back on the scalding spray. As the water pummels my aching shoulders, I close my eyes, allowing visions of Hailey's tight nipples and wide eyes to dance across my mental screen. I replay the moment when that soft, aroused moan escaped her lips, again and again, until my balls ache and my cock is as hard as it was in that moment before she ran, when I was so certain she was going to let me take her hand and show her all the new fun we could have together.

In my imagination, I change the ending to tonight's story...

Hailey's arms drop to her sides and her head falls back, bringing her lips closer to mine as she whispers, "Teach me."

"I will teach you, sweetheart, but first I need to show your breasts how much I've missed them," I say, fisting my hands at the bottom of her shirt.

A moment later, I've ripped the soft fabric over her head, baring her beautiful breasts and those rose-petal pink nipples that have slain me since the moment I first laid eyes on them. "Meet me in the bedroom," I say, voice husky as I brush my thumb over first one puckered tip and then the other, balls clenching even tighter as Hailey's eyes flood with desire. "On your back, arms over your head."

"Yes, sir," she says, her use of the honorific enough to make my hands shake as I slap her ass and order, "Bedroom. Now."

After locking the door behind me and fetching thick, soft rope from my bag, I join her in the darkened room at the back of the apartment, humming in approval as I see her stretched out wearing nothing but a pair of white bikini panties. Her arms are already stretched over her head, accentuating the upward curve of her breasts.

"Perfect. Beautiful," I murmur as I toe off my shoes and join her on the bed, bending to press a soft kiss to first one breast and then the other before reaching for her wrists. "We'll start slow, Curious. No pain. I'm going to break you with

pleasure this time. Make you beg for me to end your sweet suffering. Are you ready?"

"Yes, sir." Her chest rises and falls faster as I bind her wrists to each other and then to the bed. "I've missed you so much. I want you so much."

"Me, too," I confess as I roll on top of her.

"Yes," she says, wrapping her legs around my waist. "Break me, Will. Make me beg, make it so good it hurts."

And so I do. I palm her breasts, teasing her nipples between my fingers before dropping my head to kiss and lick and suck her honeyed skin deep into my mouth. I bite and flick, tease and torment, ravishing her breasts until her skin is swollen and red and every other sound out of her mouth is a whimper.

Finally, she breaks with a sob, tears slipping from her eyes as she pleads with me to take her, to fuck her, to "Please, oh, God. Oh, Will, please let me come. Please make me come. Please... I need you inside me so badly. I'm going to die if you don't—"

Her words end in a ragged cry of relief as I tug the crotch of her panties roughly to one side and drive into her to the hilt, so desperate to be buried inside her I can't wait the five extra seconds it would take to strip the fabric down her thighs.

Fisting one hand in her hair as the other grips her ass tight, I fuck her hard, owning her pussy with each brutal thrust, staking my claim as she comes, her sweetness locking down on my cock, so wet and tight and—

I come with a groan that echoes off the shower walls, my cock jerking in my hand as my release rushes hot and thick between my fingers. I brace myself on the cool shower wall and ride out the waves of my orgasm, feeling lonely now that reality has swept in to banish Fantasy Hailey to the far reaches of my imagination.

But it's for the best.

That Hailey isn't real, at least not yet. And if tonight's aborted Lesson One is anything to judge by, it might be a damned long time until she's ready for me to tie her up, let alone for her to beg me to break her with pleasure.

And then there's the matter of the other man in her life, this mystery dick fungus in human form who incited her curiosity about submission in the first place.

Thinking about him makes me start itching beneath the skin all over again, banishing the soothing effects of the bourbon and steamy shower.

I dry off with rough swipes of the towel across my sensitized skin, jaw clenched tight at the unwelcome image of Hailey kneeling at this mystery douche nozzle's feet. It enrages and devastates in equal measure.

If only I'd been honest with her. If only I'd confessed how much I wanted to control her pleasure, this might never have happened. We might never have separated or lost an entire year of the life we should be living together. She might be waiting for me in bed right now, smelling like honeysuckle and mint from the ointment she rubbed on a sore shoulder after her shower, ready to make love or play games or just snuggle and talk through our day until we're both tired enough to go to sleep.

I miss her voice in the darkness as much as I miss

her body close to mine. I miss waking up with her knees in my back because she could never stay on her side of the bed. I miss the way she would laugh in her sleep and how happy it made me to know my girl was that content—so free and easy that even her dreams were sweet.

As I tug on a pair of boxer briefs and stretch out on top of the covers, my chest feels like a volcano exploded near my heart. I feel cratered, blown open, as pain-filled and vulnerable as I did when Hailey and I first split and I wasn't sure how I was going to survive losing her.

Our lessons haven't even started, and they're already ripping open old wounds. If I had any sense of self-preservation at all, I would end this now—call Hailey and tell her it's clearly not working out and that we should go back to being business partners who communicate through our accountant and forget this crazy coincidence ever happened.

But it did happen.

Out of all the hundreds of thousands of people in the greater Portland area, a personal ad brought me back to the only woman I've ever loved. It can't be just a coincidence. It means something. It means that Hailey and I belong together—we just need to work a little harder to make it to happily ever after.

I'm not afraid of hard work. I'm not afraid of failure, either. The only thing worse than failing to win Hailey back would be to never get in the ring to fight for her in the first place. If I fail, I fail, but I'm not going to spend the rest of my life wondering "what if."

I'm going to leave it all on the ice, all at her feet, all

laid bare for this woman who still means everything to me, no matter how many months we've spent apart.

Finally, after a good hour of tossing and turning, I fall asleep and dream of Hailey smiling up at me in the sunlight, promising that we're going to make up for all our lost time.

CHAPTER 6

"*A*nd then what happened?" Sabrina's green eyes are nearly as big around as my fists, and I'm pretty sure she's going to fall off her stationary bike if she leans any closer to mine.

But considering this spin class is being held in the shallow end of the YMCA pool, the most damage my sister would sustain is a soaked sports bra and some smeared eyeliner. Bree may have given up modeling, but she's still not about to step foot outside her apartment without eyeliner and mascara, even if she's only headed to the gym.

"Jesus, woman, spill it!" she hisses. "Don't keep me in suspense."

Casting a furtive glance toward the front of the class, where our no-nonsense underwater bicycling teacher is shouting encouragement over the music, urging us to "push through the resistance, little fishies, you've got this!" I shake my head. "Then nothing happened. I froze. I freaked out. I bailed."

Sabrina's pert nose wrinkles. "So you ran out of your own apartment in the middle of the night?"

I roll my eyes. "No, I faked an emergency and hid in the bathroom until Will left."

"You faked an..." Sabrina breaks off with a snort-giggle. "Oh my God, you didn't. Tell me you didn't fake a case of the green apple splatters to avoid sex lessons."

"I couldn't think of anything else," I say defensively, scowling as Bree begins laughing so hard her feet slip off the pedals. "What? It was the first thing that popped into my head. Will knows I'm allergic to eggs, and I knew I had frozen custard in the freezer from the last time you came over, so..."

Sabrina laughs harder, her eyes squeezing shut as she braces her forearms on her handlebars. "Well, that's one way to kill the mood."

"Will and I lived together for five years, Bree, it's not like he's laboring under the impression that I never do number two."

Bree snorts, coughs, and ends up choking on her next round of hysterical giggles, finally drawing the attention of Kyle, our instructor.

"Focus, girls!" he shouts, snapping his fingers over his head. "Mermaids don't earn their legs by slacking off halfway to the finish line."

"Mermaids..." Sabrina gasps for air as a fresh wave of laughter makes her shoulders shake. "How is a mermaid going to ride a bicycle?"

"Let's push this, ladies!" Kyle shouts, ignoring

Sabrina as he stands on his pedals, lifting his purple-speedo-covered bottom out of the water. "Ramp up your resistance and let's go, go, go!"

Attempting to pull herself together, Sabrina brings her hands back into position, pedaling diligently even as soft snorts of laughter continue to escape. A part of me wants to reach over and pinch her thigh under the water, the way I would have when we were kids and she had one of her epic giggle fits, but the logical part of me realizes that she's simply too young to understand.

I'm only two years older than her twenty-one, but the things I went through as a kid made me grow up fast. And I was in a serious relationship with a full-grown man for five years. I understand that it's impossible to maintain a sense of girlish mystery when you're sharing a home—and a bathroom—with the one you love.

Will held my hair back when I vomited on my twenty-first birthday—even two mai tais were one too many for this lightweight—gave me a bath when I had the flu and was too weak to drag my body out of bed, and ran to the pharmacy when I would start my period and realize I was out of tampons. He knows I once had a case of athlete's foot that lasted two months, that I smell terrible after a hard workout, and that eating anything with eggs in it is going to send me racing for the bathroom.

He knows every flawed, human, stinky, not-perfectly-feminine part of me, and he still loved me to bits and pieces anyway.

He still *loves* me anyway...

I could feel it last night. Love was there in the room, simmering beneath the sexual tension that thickened the air, making every breath feel loaded with dangerous possibilities.

Dangerous, but exciting, too...

That's what had scared me the most—how much I liked the thought of taking Lesson One even further, of stripping off my clothes and letting Will do whatever wicked things he wanted to do to my body. He was right —there was a reason I'd skipped the bra as I was getting dressed for a night in. I hadn't realized it at the time, but my subconscious knew what it wanted.

After a year of celibacy, my subconscious is sick of nights spent in bed with a naughty book and my vibrator. My subconscious wants skin on skin, heat on heat, and Will back in my bed, however that needs to happen. If he wants to tie me up and torture me until I beg him to end my erotic suffering—so be it.

I shiver despite the warm water and the heat building in my muscles as we push hard for the last five minutes of class. I'm not only willing to endure such a thing, I'm intrigued by the possibility of being at Will's mercy.

More than intrigued.

I *want* that, I realized last night once Will left and the panic began to fade. I want more than knowledge. I want experience. I want to dive into this headfirst.

Yes, I might end up bruised and battered, but diving in is the only way I'm going to know if Will and I can really make this work.

I want to talk to Sabrina about my realization, to see what she thinks about lessons that involve less talk and more action, but my sister is clearly not going to be a font of wisdom on this particular subject. Bree is a clever, focused, compassionate human being, but she's also a virgin who's never been in a serious relationship. There's only so much advice she's capable of giving, and I'm way too shy to talk about this kind of thing with anyone else.

Bree and I aren't just sisters—we're best friends and have been since she was old enough to hold on to the waistband of my jeans so she could toddle behind me as I trekked to the sandbox our dad had built us in the backyard. No one in the world knows me like Bree.

Besides, most of my other friends are married to Will's teammates. And though I could ask them to keep things confidential, I know how intimate relationships work. Sooner or later Diana or Amanda would let something slip to their husbands, and Will would end up getting ribbed at work for being a kinky bastard. And though I know he could handle the teasing—he's survived almost a decade in the prank-infested locker rooms of the NHL and has the thick skin to prove it—I don't want to be the one to leak his carefully kept secret.

After all, it might become *our* carefully kept secret some day, if I can muster up the courage to dive in and see if the water suits me.

So I keep my mouth shut for the rest of class, pumping hard for the finish line with the other mermaids, even as I vow never to come back to underwater spin class. Some combinations are meant to be—chocolate and peanut butter, kites and surfboards, movies and popcorn—and some are best enjoyed separately.

"Sorry," Bree says as we turn down the resistance for the cool down. "The giggle fit is under control. I'm going to be mature now. Tell me all about your evening spent locked in a bathroom. How did you and Will leave things?"

I shake my head. "It's fine. Forget about it."

"No, really, I'm good now. I won't act like I'm twelve, I promise."

I wave a dismissive hand. "Seriously, it's cool. I've thought things through and formed a plan of action."

Bree's lips turn down as she pouts. "Now I'm sad. I've let you down. I'm sorry."

"You haven't let me down," I say with a laugh. "Now tell me about your night. Did you end up going out with the guy who was raised in the commune?"

"I did. Unfortunately." Bree's green eyes roll toward the ceiling. "I swear to God, the next guy who says he's thirty and shows up wearing Birkenstocks from when he used to follow Phish and spray-on hair to cover his bald spot is going to get a swift kick in the shins. If I wanted to date someone old enough to be my dad, I would have set my preferences to include 'older than dirt.'"

I grin. "Aw, come on. You know you have a thing for canned toupee hair. It's like silly string, but for grown-ups."

"It is nothing like silly string," Bree says, decidedly

unamused. "Silly string is fun. Wig whiz is an abomination. And you have no idea how hard it is out there in the dating-app jungle. I did end up connecting with this other guy after I dumped the Crypt-Keeper, and he was pretty interesting, but that is definitely the exception, not the rule... Be glad you skipped this part of the modern mate-finding process."

"You could always do it the old-fashioned way," I say with a shrug. "Go meet someone at a bar or a club or something. Or try speed dating!"

Bree shudders, her eyes closing as she shakes her head. "Please, sister dear, don't act old. It's so sad when you act old."

"I'm not old!" I flick my fingers, splashing water on her midriff. "Speed dating is still a thing, right?"

"Sure, it's still a thing," she says, flicking water back in my direction. "And my friends and I are still churning milk to make butter in our spare time."

"Brat." I splash her with more force this time, making her gasp as water lands on her shoulder.

"Stop it. If you get my face wet and my mascara runs, I will have to kill you."

I widen my eyes and fake a terrified gasp. "Oh, no, I'm so scared. Please, scrawny former model girl, please don't hurt me with your non-existent muscles."

"That's it," Bree says, hopping off her bike. "You're going down."

"No, wait, I was just—" My words end in a gurgle as Bree tackles me, knocking me off my bike and into the water on the other side. My head goes under and my nose fills and by the time I break the surface—sputtering and coughing—I'm hell-bent on revenge.

"Ladies, please!" Kyle shouts as Bree takes off up the row of stationary bikes and I follow, hot on her trail. "Back on your bikes! Only quitters skip the cooldown."

"I'm sorry, Kyle," Bree huffs as she fights her way through the water in a slow-motion sprint. "My sister's lost it. She's snapped. I don't know what's gotten into her."

"You knocked me off my bike, you scrawny liar," I say, inspiring a wave of laughter from the rest of the class.

"It's true," a voice pipes up from the back row. "I saw it go down. The tall, skinny one started it."

"Lies!" Bree gasps in outrage, but her lips are curved at the edges. "I would never."

"Get the skinny one!" another voice calls out. "Don't let her get out of the pool without going under."

Within moments, the class has devolved into a splash war with Bree and a few of the super fit and fashionable girls from the front row on one side and us mortals of average height and fashion sense on the other. But it's a playful, giggle-fueled war, and by the time we all straggle out of the pool, we're all smiles.

"That was fun," Bree says, slinging an arm around my shoulders. "I like being ridiculous with you. Don't ever completely grow up, okay?"

"Never," I promise, meaning it with my entire heart.

I'm never going to grow out of being silly with my sister or taking part in an impromptu splash war. But it's time for me to grow beyond the anxiety that's had me tied in knots since I learned that Will is my Discreet Gentleman.

It's time to woman up and face the challenge the universe has placed in my path. No more running or hiding.

Now I just have to figure out how to tell Will I'm ready for the "hands on" version of Lesson One...

CHAPTER 7

WILL

*T*he best thing about having old fogies on our team—Brendan, our captain, and Petrov are both getting up there—is that I have solid role models to look to as I enter my thirties. And though I honestly don't feel any different than I did when I was drafted at twenty-two, I know that if I want to keep playing at the top of my game, I'm going to have to work harder to stay strong and flexible.

And so, though the last thing I want to do on this bright and beautiful Saturday morning is stick my ass into the air and breathe deeply for an hour and a half, here I am in the workout studio down the hall from the locker room, getting my downward dog on with Wallace, Petrov, and a handful of other hardcore players who aren't too sore from last night's game to make it to yoga class.

"Inhale." Stephanie, our patchouli-scented instructor pulls in a deep breath as she pads barefoot around the room between our mats, offering encouragement and making adjustments. "And as you exhale, allow your heels to drop closer to the floor. Tilt your pelvis, aiming your sit-bones toward the back wall as you draw your belly in toward your spine and allow your shoulders to sink closer to your mat. Beautiful, Shane."

"Thank you, Stephanie. I feel beautiful," Wallace says in his deep, gravelly voice, sending a ripple of laughter through the room.

"Good, then let's see if you're ready to go deeper." Stephanie, accustomed to taking shit from our goalie, places her hands on Wallace's lower back and leans in, pushing his heels closer to his mat, summoning a groan from low in his throat. "Breathe into the discomfort," Stephanie says, a peaceful, yet slightly wicked, smile curving her full lips. "Will, gaze on your navel—there's nothing to see here. Keep your focus on your own mat."

"Yes, ma'am," I murmur, inspiring another soft wave of chuckles. At five-two and maybe a hundred pounds dripping wet, Stephanie is hardly an intimidating physical specimen, but the woman rules her yoga classes with a gently padded iron fist. She is not to be toyed with, and we all do our best to give her the respect she deserves as an expert in her field—because most of us lack the flexibility to do even half the poses she demonstrates each class.

"Now shift forward into plank and hold," Stephanie says. "We'll move slowly through this first sun salutation, and then I want you to do five cycles on your own. Let your breath instigate your movement and allow it to flow through your transition from one posture to the next."

Once the self-guided portion of the class begins, I turn my attention inward, letting the moving meditation take me to that quiet, focused place I first accessed on the ice. Entering the flow state during games—that domain where body and mind are completely in sync and working almost effortlessly together toward a goal —is what hooked me on hockey for life. Later, I realized that state of harmony was available to me in other places, too. In the bedroom, for example, with a submissive woman who knows how to let power exchange work its magic on both of us.

For me, Domination isn't just about control or even hot sex; it's about tapping into something primal and true, something as powerful as the utterly peaceful place I've been lucky enough to visit a few times in Stephanie's class.

Today, though, I already know I won't be reaching anything close to nirvana.

Even as I focus on the asana, the scene at Hailey's apartment last night plays on repeat inside my decidedly un-peaceful mind. She was so close to embracing the experience. But instead of easing into the flow, she ran from me, the same way she did the night I proposed.

Up until last September, I'd never known Hailey to be a runner. I mean, she literally goes jogging almost every day and has never met a 5k she didn't want to sign up for, but she's always faced problems head on.

When we were struggling to establish domestic bliss our first year together, Hailey was the one who insisted we sit down and talk through our grievances until we discovered a better way to cohabitate—a way that involved me taking out the trash before it started to overflow and her removing the blond squirrel from the shower drain after she washed her hair instead of leaving it there to cause plumbing problems. When our first financial advisor ignored her suggestions for our business because she was younger and female, she kindly, but firmly, let him go, and she tolerates exactly zero bullshit from her students, her employees, or the bums who hang around the relatively unsavory corner our gym calls home.

She is sweet as sunshine, but she's also tough as nails. So why did she run? From me of all people?

She has to know that I would never hurt her. Even if I had her tied up and at my mercy, I would never take a scene in a direction she hadn't given me explicit permission to pursue.

And even if she doesn't understand that yet, if her grasp on proper BDSM etiquette isn't as strong as it could be, that doesn't explain why she ran from me the night I proposed. For the thousandth time, my gut insists that there's something I'm missing about that night, a piece of the puzzle that doesn't fit.

Before I got down on one knee at the party, Hailey hadn't given the slightest sign that anything was wrong. We'd been planning a ski vacation for December, considering selling our condo to buy a house in the suburbs where we could finally get the dog we'd both been wanting, and debating whether to rent a bowling alley or an indoor trampoline park for our next joint birthday celebration—we were born on the same day, eight years apart, and took advantage of coincidence to throw a massive bash every year.

There were so many things binding us together—love, friendship, laughter, tradition, shared goals, shared dreams—so why the hell have I spent the last year alone? I'm still not buying that a need to prove she could make it on her own was enough to derail our love train.

There has to be something else. But what the fuck is it?

"Exhale, Will." Stephanie's gentle whisper and her hands on the small of my back as I push into my final downward-facing dog draw my attention to my clenched jaw. "Why don't you take child's pose for a minute and try to let go of whatever story is taking control. Let go, and come back to the intention you set at the beginning of class."

With a sigh, I sink onto my knees and rest my forehead on the floor, taking child's pose and closing my eyes, though I know focus is a lost cause at this point. As we'd sat cross-legged on our mats at the beginning of class, I'd planned to concentrate on gratitude, something that always gives me a lift when I'm feeling down. It's hard to be cranky over a missed shot or murderous over a ref's crap call when you're giving thanks for your strength, your skill, and the fact that in a world filled with suffering people you get to play a game you love for a living.

But right now, I'm having a hard time accessing a grateful headspace. Yes, I've been given more than my fair share of gifts, but what use is fame, talent, or money without someone to share it with? Without the one woman who made me feel seen, understood, and loved for who I am, not how much I make or the cool things I can make my body do on the ice.

No, I'm definitely not feeling the grateful vibe. I'm feeling frustrated and confused and on the verge of rolling off my mat and slipping quietly out the door. Maybe it would be best to bail and take my bad attitude with me, leaving the rest of my teammates to tie themselves in pretzels in peace.

I'm about to make a break for freedom when Wallace hisses, "Hey, want to grab a coffee after class? Need to get something off my chest."

I turn my head to meet his gaze beneath my outstretched arm, noting how different he looks upside down, with his bright white teeth glowing against his still summer-tan skin in the dim light of the studio. "What? Did you hit on one of my sisters again?"

Wallace rolls his eyes. "No, I don't have a death wish, asshole, and that happened way before I knew who was related to who around here. There's just something—"

"Breathe now, boys, gossip later." Stephanie steps between us, her bare feet silent on the glossy wood floor.

"Yes, teach," Wallace says. "Sorry. I just wanted to tell Saunders how inspiring I find his child's pose. He looks like a cute little baby, all curled up on his mat like that."

Chuckles fill the room, and I smile. "Thank you, Wallace. And I'm proud of you for wearing boxer briefs under your shorts today so we don't all have to get an eyeful of your hairy balls every time you take down dog."

The chuckles become full-blown waves of laughter, and before long, the entire class has fallen out of their posture and Stephanie is glaring at me with her arms crossed at her chest. But her dark eyes are dancing and her lips are curved, so I know she isn't really mad.

Hell, she's probably grateful someone finally called Wallace out so he and all the other assholes who forget to wear something tight under their gym shorts can mend their ball-flashing ways.

"Okay, since we're all in such good spirits today, we'll move right on to hip openers," Stephanie says, inspiring a groan from everyone except Wallace. As a goalie, he has to be more flexible than the rest of us.

And though I enjoy making fun of the weird frog stretch he does during warm-ups, as we move into pigeon pose, I make a note to incorporate more stretching into my pre-game routine. Within the first few seconds in pigeon, my hips are on fire and my lower back is insisting that yoga is the devil's exercise. By the time we've been in the posture for a minute—one-third the minimum time Stephanie insists we hold hip openers—the entire class is grumbling and cussing, sweating and whining and generally acting like a pack of Grade A Diaper Babies.

If our enemies on the ice could see us now, they'd never fear a Portland Badger again.

The thought ignites something deep in my brain, setting a candle to burning in the darkness. Everyone has vulnerable places they prefer to keep hidden from their enemies and sometimes even from their friends.

What if popping the question shot an arrow through a chink in Hailey's armor I hadn't suspected was there? What if she has issues with the institution of marriage for some reason, despite her parents clearly loving relationship?

Oddly enough, we had never discussed getting hitched before the day I decided to pull a ring out of my pocket. We'd discussed almost everything else—from how many kids we wanted to the best places to retire when we were old and gray but still in great shape because we would refuse to let ourselves go—but not the actual "I do" process. I had simply expected that marriage was something that would happen before we decided to start our family.

And though it's a cliché, I know that assuming often *does* make an ass out of "U" and me. It's always better to communicate than to assume.

Maybe that's all this is. Maybe Hailey's afraid of getting married, or morally against the institution for some reason, and that's what sent us veering off course. Maybe that's why she ran last night, too—not because she wasn't into the idea of having play time, but because she realized play time might lead us down a road that ends in a big commitment, sooner or later.

The idea swims around in my head, growing larger and more fully formed as the class rolls on. By the time we reach savasana and are granted the sweet relief of lying in corpse pose for the oh-so-relaxing last ten minutes of class, I've decided the theory is worth putting to the test.

But how?

I'm still noodling on that when class ends, Stephanie thanks us for the opportunity to serve us on our yoga journey—she seems to mean it every time, the sweetheart—and we all roll off our mats to gather our things.

I've totally forgotten about Wallace and his need to unburden himself until he jabs me in the ribs with his rolled-up yoga mat and asks, "Still up for coffee? Or we can just take the long way to the parking lot if you don't have time to caffeinate."

"Sure, let's walk, what's up?" I fall in beside him as he starts for the door, pausing to high-five my teammates on the way. We're a close group, those of us man enough to admit we need some yoga in our life—and in our aching joints—and I always feel closer to them after our ninety minutes of mindful torture.

But I always feel close to Wallace. I took him under my wing when he was drafted three years ago—the kid was so nervous during his first practice I knew someone had to hold his hand or he wouldn't make it a month as a Badger—and we've been good friends ever since. Once he felt comfortable enough to relax, Wallace turned out to be hilarious and have a heart as big as his bear-like body.

I consider him an honorary little brother, one I often like more than my biological brother, Jacob, who lives to stress my parents out with his latest get-rich-quick scheme or plan to hitchhike across Canada in the middle of winter.

"It's about Sabrina, Hailey's sister?" Wallace crosses his arms over his mat, pinning it to his chest with an anxious look that makes me arch a brow.

"Yeah, I know Sabrina. And I'm aware that she's Hailey's sister. What about her?"

Wallace laughs uncomfortably. "Yeah, right, well... So, I ran into her last night outside of Voodoo Donuts at, like, two in the morning. Some friends and I were looking for something to soak up the beer, ended up grabbing a table next to Sabrina's, and I got a good look at the dude she was hanging out with..."

I nod. "Looked like bad news?"

"Oh, he is absolutely bad news." Wallace's shakes his head. "This guy is a confirmed douchebag of the highest order. He was dating my friend Cane's twin sister Cami for six months. He cheated on her non-stop, wrecked her car and refused to pay for the repairs, and gave her a nasty case of crabs before he dumped her for another girl on her birthday."

"Repulsive," I observe. "He sounds like a shit weasel, but you don't have to worry about Sabrina. She's not the type to suffer fools. She'll realize he's full of shit and dump his ass before things get too serious."

Wallace pulls a face. "I don't know, she looked pretty into him last night and... Well, the guy is a loser, but he's also good-looking. Like John Travolta-in-his-heyday good-looking."

I smirk. "John Travolta?"

"Yes, John Travolta," Wallace says, his blue eyes narrowing. "He was a smoking hot dude when he was young, and this guy is like that. Big pouty lips and cheekbones for days and stubble on his chin and skinny, hipster-sized muscles popping out under his tiny T-shirts and shit."

"Sounds like you've studied your man-crush closely," I tease, making Wallace scowl harder.

"Dude, I'm just trying to communicate to you that the guy is lady kryptonite. Even smart ladies are helpless against him. Cami is a vet, and you have to be smart as fuck to be a vet. It's even harder than being a doctor, because you have to heal a multitude of creatures, not just humans, and she still got used hard by this player."

"Okay, I hear you," I say, sobering. "So you want me to warn Sabrina? Drop her a line and say I've heard some not-great stuff about her latest hookup?"

Wallace's scowl melts into relief. "Yeah, would you? Bree and I are friends, but I didn't want to be the one to drop the douchebag bomb. She would probably think I was just jealous or something and not take me seriously. But if it comes from a guy who's like her brother, she'll know the warning is for real."

"What's the douchebag's name?" I ask, ignoring the pang that flashes through my chest as I wonder if Sabrina still considers me "like a brother" material. We've texted a few times since Hailey and I broke up, but we aren't nearly as close as we were before. When I lost Hailey, I didn't just lose my other half, I lost her family, too, and unlike a lot of my friends, I actually liked my potential in-laws.

"Creedence," Wallace says, laughing when I pull a face. "Right? Pretentious as fuck. And if that's the name on his birth certificate, I will eat my own jock strap after the next game."

My wince deepens as we step out into the mid-morning sun. "Don't make that bet. Just in case."

Wallace grins. "I will totally make that bet. You know I live on the edge, and there's nothing I won't eat, especially on a dare. Speaking of eating, are you starving? I'm always starving after yoga. Who knew stretching worked up such an appetite? Want to grab breakfast burritos? Extra cheese, extra beans, my treat?"

"Thanks, but I've actually got somewhere to be." I lift a hand as I head east and Wallace breaks west toward downtown. "See you Monday."

He points his rolled-up mat at my chest. "See you. And thanks, man. I appreciate your help with the Sabrina thing."

"No problem," I say as I start toward my truck, my thoughts tumbling.

A douchebag intervention with Sabrina isn't just a good excuse to touch base with a friend I haven't talked to in a while. It might also be a way to gain some insight into Hailey's views on marriage. I would never try to manipulate Sabrina into intervening on my behalf, but there's nothing wrong with gathering information.

Now I just have to figure out how to do that without looking like a sad sack who's still obsessing over my failed proposal a year after Hailey and I called it quits. Tugging my phone out of my bag, I chew the inside of my lip for a moment and then decide it's best not to overthink things. The right words will come to me in the moment. They always do.

I shoot off a quick text to Bree. *Hey, what's up? Can you hop on the phone for a few minutes? I promised a friend I would give you a stern talking to about your date last night.*

Only a few seconds later, Bree responds. *Which one? The guy with silly string for hair? Or my bad boy with the soft and gooey artistic center?*

With a grunt, I tap out: *I'm guessing the bad boy, since option one doesn't sound like he has much luck with the ladies. You got a few minutes?*

By the time I reach my truck, my phone buzzes and Bree's contact info pops up on the screen. I answer with a smile. "Hey there, slugger. How's it going?"

"Pretty good until now," Bree says. "Why do I need a stern talking to about Creedence? He's so yummy, Will. And nice and funny and he paid for my donut instead of asking for separate checks. Do you know how rare that is in this day and age? I can't remember the last time a guy offered to pay for something."

"Then you're clearly dating the wrong guys."

Bree snorts. "Obviously. That's why I'm still single after seven months of online dating like it's my job. But Creedence is different than the other bozos. He has amazing fluffy, black, 80s rocker hair like Uncle Jesse on *Full House*." She lets out a dreamy sigh that makes me laugh.

"That's better than John Travolta, I guess."

"What?"

"Nothing," I say, not wanting to give Wallace away. "I hate to burst your bubble, but I heard from a reliable source that Creedence is a douche canoe. Apparently he wrecked his last girlfriend's car and refused to pay for the repairs, cheated on her like it was *his* job, and gave her an STD as a break-up present."

Sabrina lets out a moan so loud it makes me pull my phone away from my ear. "Nooooo, not an STD!! But he's so cute! And when we split our second donut, he let me have the half with more icing and sugar loops on it."

"That's disgusting, Bree. Sugary cereals are poison on their own, let alone added to a deep-fried donut."

"Oh, stop. If I listened to you and Hailey, all I would ever eat is kale, quinoa, and organic mushroom supplements. She wants to talk to you, by the way. Here, talk to her while I drown my despair in my cappuccino."

Before I can prepare myself for the shift in gears, Hailey is on the line, her voice soft and husky. "Hey, thanks for the heads up on the creep. I was just telling Bree that she should try to meet someone the old-fashioned way. She told me I was old."

I hear Sabrina shout "so old!" in the background and smile. "You're not old," I assure Hailey. "You're an old soul with a good head on your shoulders. Big difference."

"I'll tell her that, though I'm sure she won't listen. Be right back, Bree." Hailey pauses, and I hear a chair scrape across a hardwood floor then footsteps before she continues in a softer voice. "So, I've been thinking a lot about last night..."

"Me, too," I say, my pulse picking up. I start to apologize for pushing her, but stop myself, wanting to hear what she has to say first.

"Yeah, well..." Hailey clears her throat. "I'm sorry for freaking out and hiding in the bathroom. That was a cowardly way to express my anxiety about the situation."

"It's all right," I say, hopes plummeting. But I suppose it's better to end this now rather than two or three lessons in when reconciliation might have actually seemed within reach. "If it doesn't feel right, it doesn't feel right. You shouldn't force yourself to do something you don't want to do."

"But that's the thing..." She sighs, the wistful sound making my chest ache. "I don't know that it felt right, necessarily, but it didn't feel wrong, either. And I was definitely...curious."

"Yeah?" My pulse speeds again as I toss my bag into the truck bed. "How curious?"

"So curious that I lay awake in bed for hours after you left, cursing myself for being such a big baby. And that's when I realized that I don't want what I asked for in my personal ad. I want...more."

"How much more?" I ask, my voice deeper, huskier.

"Like you said. I want the full experience. The hands-on experience," she says, making my cock thicken. "That's the only way I'm ever going to know for sure if this is right for me. But I confess I'm still a little scared."

"There's no reason to be scared." The ache in my chest spreads to tighten my throat. "You know I would never hurt you, Hailey. Not ever."

"I know," she whispers. "But I'm still nervous. What if I... What if I stink at it?"

My lips curve. "You won't stink at it. That's impossible. You're good at everything you do."

"Not playing the piano. After three years my teacher begged my parents to stop bringing me to lessons, even though they were her only clients that paid on time. She was *that* desperate to be spared any more of my rhythm-challenged stabbing and plunking."

"I didn't know you played the piano."

"I didn't know you liked tying women up and spanking them," she says, her breath rushing out before she adds, "Sorry. I didn't mean that. At least not the way it sounded."

"It's okay." I lean against the sun-warmed side of the truck, gazing at the leaves turning red and gold at the edge of the parking lot. They're beautiful, but they're also a reminder that summer doesn't last forever, that windows of opportunity close, and that a man puts off until tomorrow what should be done today at his peril. So I screw my courage to the sticking point and say, "I'm sorry about that, Hailey. I'm sorry I hid that part of myself from you."

"Yeah… Why did you do that?" she asks in a small voice that makes it clear how much my secrecy hurt her. "I always thought we shared everything. It was something I loved about us, that we were honest with each other. Even when it was scary and hard."

"I know. I loved that about us, too," I say, feeling like shit. "I had my reasons at the time, but…" I shake my head. "Now they seem pretty stupid and short-sighted. Especially in light of you meeting some other guy who's made you curious about the lifestyle." Jealousy makes me feel sour from the inside out. "Speaking of Mystery Guy, how is he going to feel about you going for the full experience with your ex? Is he the kind who likes to share his subs?"

"Are you?" she asks, dodging the question.

"No, I don't. But there are men who like to sub swap or have their submissive sleep with other men as a way of testing their obedience. That's something you'll want to find out about before you get in too deep with this guy."

"I'm not worried about that right now," she says, her tone making it clear she's as uncomfortable with this topic as I am. "You know I like to take life one day at a time. Right now I just want to learn the ropes and see if I like them."

Oh, she'll like them. I'm going to make sure of it. And then I'm going to make sure that she likes it even more, so much that she won't be able to imagine letting any man top her but me.

"Are you free tonight?" I ask. I would prefer to meet her wherever she and Bree are having coffee, throw her over my shoulder, and carry her to the nearest hotel. But I need to take things slow this time and do my best not to trigger Hailey's flight instinct.

"I am. Want to come over and give Lesson One another shot?"

Hell, yes, I do, but if we start the night alone, the chances that I'll be able to keep my cool and my hands to myself long enough to put Hailey at ease are slim to fucking none.

"I have a better idea," I say, inspiration striking as I push away from the truck to pace back and forth in the rapidly emptying parking lot. "Let's start with a field trip. I'll swing by and pick you up outside your building around six?"

"That works. And a field trip sounds exciting," she says, a smile in her voice. "I'll be looking forward to it, but I should probably get going now. Bree is giving me the stink eye. We're supposed to be bonding over brunch, and I left her alone at our table. If I don't get back soon, I'm risking salt in my cappuccino."

"Go. Bond. Brunch, and I'll see you soon."

"Soon," she echoes. "And thanks again for looking out for my little sis. I'll make sure she gives STD guy the hard boot."

"You do that. She deserves better." I say goodbye and end the call, but as I slide into the truck and head for home, my last words to Hailey keep circling through my head.

Bree does deserve better, but so does Hailey. She deserves better than this mystery asshole she's got her eye on. Even if he's the classiest, cleanest, most boundary-respecting Dom in Portland, he won't love her the way I do. He couldn't.

Hailey and I have a history—a damn good one—and the kind of love that never should have become past tense. She deserves a Dominant lover who adores her, who would break every bone in his own hand before he would push her too far or take liberties she isn't ready to give.

She deserves me, and I deserve a second chance to prove I'm the only man who should ever worship at the altar of her incomparable pussy.

The thought makes a rush of heat sweep across my

skin. I can't think about her pussy or how incredible it feels to be inside her or how much I'm dying to make love to her again. I have to keep my thoughts on my lesson plan and my eye on the prize. First I'll remind Hailey that I'm still someone she can trust with her life, let alone her heart, and then I'll refresh her memory on how well we work together in the bedroom.

Yes, we'll be adding a new element into our sexual relationship, but Hailey isn't the kind to back down from a challenge. Now all I have to do is show her how fun and sexy this particular challenge has the potential to be...

CHAPTER 8

From the text messages of Hailey Marks and William Saunders

Hailey: Hey! I was wondering if we were going to grab dinner out or if I should eat before we go?

William: You should eat something before we go, and I'll bring some snacks, too. I'm not sure if where we're going has food or not.

Hailey: Well, if you give me our destination details, I could check that out…

William: No way, woman. Tonight is for surprises.

Hailey: All right, but are they fancy surprises or casual surprises? I love a mystery as much as the next girl, but I don't want to get in trouble for being underdressed again.

William: Jeans and a T-shirt will be fine, but bring a jacket. The nights are getting colder, and we'll be outside for most of the evening.

Hailey: Gotcha. And what about a bra? Should I wear one of those?

William: If you would like to avoid getting ravished the second you climb into the truck, I would advise it. There are limits to even my self-control, sweetheart.

Hailey: I'll take that under advisement, sir.

William: I told you, I'm not into the "sir" thing full time. I like to top in the bedroom, but most of the time I'm just me. No special treatment required.

Hailey: I know. I was just testing the "sir" out…
Seeing how it feels…

William: And how does it feel, Curious?

Hailey: It feels good, Discreet.
Exciting. Sexy.

William: Maybe you shouldn't put on that bra, after all…

Hailey: LOL. I'm putting on a bra. I'm excited about our field trip and don't want us to be late. Besides, we have time. We're only two days into our six-week course.

William: True. But time flies when you're having fun. I want you to have fun tonight, okay? Just relax and go with the flow and let me take the lead. I'll take care of you, no matter what. I promise.

Hailey: You always do.
See in you in an hour?

William: See you then, sexy.
Oh, and Hailey…

Hailey: Yes, Will?

William: Your safe word is ninja.

Hailey: Am I going to need a safe word tonight?

William: Not sure, but I believe in being prepared.

Hailey: I know you do. It's one of the things I like best about you.
Off to write "ninja" on a Post-It note so I won't forget ;).

William: You won't forget.

Hailey: You're right. I won't. See you soon, sir.

William: Soon, Cat.

CHAPTER 9

HAILEY

I was never bored with Will.

Even after we'd been together for years and had fallen into comfortable patterns and relationship routines, he had a way of keeping me guessing. Every once and a while, out of nowhere, he would do something unpredictable, reminding me that I might never completely know this amazing man, but making me grateful that I would have a lifetime to try.

Sometimes it would be something silly like starting a water balloon fight on our balcony at the end of a sweltering summer day. Other times it would be heartbreakingly sweet, like bringing home bulbs to plant in my mother's garden to help my family celebrate seven cancer-free years.

He would show up at the gym after practice in full fishing gear and declare that he was teaching me how to fly fish—after never having mentioned going fishing a single day in his life—or recite a Shakespearean sonnet from memory while we were on our way to see theater in the park. He made my jaw drop and my eyebrows shoot up on a regular basis, but back when we were a couple I thought I had a pretty good handle on who Will was beneath the surprises.

Now, as I pace back and forth in front of my building, wondering if I'm overdressed in a pair of boot-cut jeans, a pink button-up peasant shirt, and a brown crocheted vest with fringe trim that my sister assured me was fashionable and not "too hippy cowgirl," I have no idea what to expect.

What kind of surprise has Dominant Will cooked up in that creative brain of his?

Where is he taking me? What are we going to do? And how is he going to pull off a submissive lesson while we're out in public?

A part of me—the part that likes rules, schedules, and routines—is anxious.

But the rest of me...

I bounce lightly on my toes, willing the minute hand to move faster.

The rest of me is giddy, flushed, fizzing, and alive in a way I haven't felt in a long time. I can't wait to find out what Will has in store for us tonight. But even more than that, I can't wait to kiss him again, touch him again.

I can't wait to feel his body hot against mine and his arms holding me close, and to finally stop pretending that I'm fine with being "just friends."

Just friends is never going to work for Will and me. I can't be around him for more than a minute without thinking about how incredible he looks, how nice he smells, or all the ways I would touch him if that wasn't currently off-limits.

For nearly a year, it has been. For nearly a year, his body has been like a piece of art in a museum—look, don't touch.

But not tonight. Tonight I will be able to touch him, taste him, get lost in the giddy nirvana of being close to the man I love.

All I have to do is wait for permission like a good submissive.

I shiver at the thought, liking it more than I ever imagined I would. A second later, Will's truck pulls into the roundabout in front of my building, and the passenger's side window rolls down. Inside, Will is smiling down at me in the fading light. "Hey, beautiful? You looking for a ride?"

"Yes, sir, I am," I say, shivering again as hunger flashes in Will's eyes. I don't know if I'll love playing the submissive as much as he enjoys playing Master, but I have to admit that I love what that word does to him.

I climb into the truck, losing my battle against a grin when Will says, "Now you're armed and dangerous, aren't you? Now that you know three little letters are all it takes to drive me out of my damned mind?"

I shake my head, smiling so wide my jaw aches a little. "No, of course not. I'm not dangerous. I'm as harmless as they come."

Will grunts. "And I'm a ballerina in my spare time."

The mental image makes me laugh as he pulls out of the drive onto Salmon Street. "I would pay good money to see that. How's yoga going, by the way? Have you touched your toes yet?"

"Not even close," he says with a chuckle. "But I enjoy trying. I am excelling at tree pose, though. Got my branches up over my head and balanced for the entire minute earlier today."

"I'm not surprised." I shift in my seat to watch him drive, loving the way his forearm muscles flex beneath the cuffed sleeves of his white button-down. "You're actually very graceful for a guy."

He snorts.

"You are," I insist. "You're poetry on the ice and when you spar with the kids at the gym. You even drive gracefully."

Will cuts a glance my way as he pulls onto the highway. "Thanks." Our eyes connect and heat flashes through me, making my cheeks feel too warm. I want to lunge across the cab and press a kiss to his cheek, the way I would have this time last year, before I learned the truth about Will. Instead, I clear my throat and force out a soft, "You're welcome," before settling into my seat to enjoy the drive as we cross the river and Will takes an exit leading out into the country.

Will is steering the ship tonight. Will decides when, where, what, and how far things go. Will is in control. My job is to wait for his signal and follow his lead.

As a person who was branded Type A in kindergarten and a Natural Leader by second grade, this should be driving me crazy. Instead, the knowledge that I don't have to call any of the shots makes me feel lighter than I have in weeks. I feel free, unencumbered, liberated by all the choices I won't have the option to make.

Maybe you'll be a good submissive after all.

The thought makes my cheeks burn hotter and I let out a giddy laugh-sigh.

"What's funny?" Will asks.

I shake my head as I turn to him, heart skipping a beat at the tenderness in his gaze as he divides his attention between the road and me. "Nothing's funny. I'm just excited. About tonight."

"Me, too," he says, eyes sparkling. "But you're about to be even more excited. Take a look over there."

"A corn maze?" I ask, reading the small, hand-painted billboard on the side of the road as Will slows down to make the next turn. "Is that where we're going?"

He grins. "What better place to teach you how to follow directions?"

I furrow my brow, briefly wondering how that's going to play out, but after only a moment I sink back into follower mode. Whatever Will has planned, my job is to go with the flow. Besides, it's a beautiful fall evening and there's nothing I love more than a corn maze, preferably followed by a hayride.

And I trust Will. No matter what happens, I'll be safe. There's no doubt in my mind.

So I smile and say, "sounds good," as I lean forward, admiring the scarecrows lining the edge of the field. Each one is styled like a different vintage horror movie monster. There's a vampire scarecrow, a mummy, a werewolf, a swamp creature, Frankenstein's monster, and a gigantic salmon with razor-sharp teeth.

"A fish," Will says, arching a brow at the salmon.

"Not just any fish. That's Gary, the killer King Salmon. He lives in the Willamette and crawls up onto the beach to feed on people foolish enough to fall asleep in the shade too close to the river."

"This is a real thing? Or something you made up?" Will pulls into a parking spot in the mostly-open field. There are only a few other trucks scattered about, making it clear most people don't consider the end of September corn maze season just yet.

"Totally real," I say. "The girls in my intermediate class were telling me about him last year at the gym Halloween party. Some people say Gary used to be a Native American warrior who, after his tribe was wiped out by smallpox, asked to be reincarnated as a giant, razor-toothed salmon so he could wreak his vengeance upon the white man who killed his family and stole his land. Others say Gary is descended from a logger from the early days of Rose City, who was so desperate for a wife that he fell in love with a fish that lived near his houseboat, married her, and made a bunch of murderous half human-half fish babies that later went crazy after exposure to toxic chemicals dumped in the water. And Tina said that Gary was a drummer from a punk band in the 70s who took some bad heroin that turned him into a salmon and that's why you should never do drugs."

"Which story do you subscribe to?" Will asks as he shuts off the truck.

"The love story, of course," I murmur, unable to keep from flirting, just a little bit. "You know I'm a sucker for a love story."

"Even if the love story ends with the creation of a giant killer fish?"

I shrug. "No love story is perfect."

"No, they aren't." Will's lips curve in a smile so sexy it makes me shiver. "Cold?"

I shake my head. "Nope."

"If you are, you can have my jacket. But first, let me help you with this." He pulls a rolled length of fabric from his pocket and takes it by one end, holding it up as it unfurls to reveal what is unmistakably a blindfold.

A thick, sturdy one that will ensure I can't see a damned thing.

Anxiety spikes in my bloodstream—I'm not a fan of not being able to see where I'm going—but I nod. "All right. I'm game."

"You're sure? You don't have to do anything you don't want to do tonight, Hailey. You know that right?"

"I know, but I was just thinking how much I trust you, so..." I tuck my hair behind my ears and shift closer to him as he lifts the blindfold. I close my eyes, heart beating faster as he guides the fabric into place and knots it firmly. "But we're keeping this G-rated for now, right?" I ask as darkness falls. "Just in case there are any kids loose in this maze?"

"Completely G-rated," Will assures me, his hand covering mine. "This is about building trust. I want you to know that when we're in a scene, you can count on me to be there for you, to take care of you, no matter what."

My tongue slips out to dampen my lips. "I already know that. I trust you, Will. I promise I do."

"Good," he says softly. "But this is also about learning to follow orders without second-guessing me or yourself. Are you ready to follow orders, Curious Cat?"

I swallow. "I think so?"

Will clucks his tongue disapprovingly. "That's not the answer I want, Kitten. The game starts now, so what do you say when I ask if you're ready to follow orders?"

"Yes, sir," I say, electricity zipping across my skin as Will makes a husky sound of approval low in his throat.

"Good, then get out of the truck, shut the door behind you, and await your next order, sweetheart. We're going to see how good you are at playing follow the leader."

"I'm going to be so good at it, sir," I say, the playful note in my voice surprising me.

But then, Will is the one who keeps calling it all a 'game' and games are meant to be fun, aren't they? So as I reach for the door, I don't fight the smile on my face or the giggle that escapes from my lips as I step out of the truck only to realize the ground is a good six-inches lower than I assumed.

And when Will joins me after locking up the truck and says, "Good work, Curious. Now I want you to take ten big steps forward." I offer a sassy salute in response. And yes, my heart is pounding as I stride across unseen ground into unexplored territory, with nothing but

Will's voice to guide me. But it isn't fear making my pulse pound.

Or at least, not only fear...

As we move into the maze, Will's commands grow more demanding—"Three big steps, then turn left for four and right for two." "Jog forward until I tell you to stop." "Run toward the sound of my voice as fast as you can."— and I realize that the fear isn't an unwanted side effect or something to be shoved aside and ignored as I soldier through to the next challenge.

The fear is...part of the fun.

Placing my safety in Will's hands sharpens my awareness, my anticipation, my elation as I sprint toward the sound of his voice only for him to sweep me off my feet and into his arms, spinning us both in a circle as we laugh like fools.

"I get it," I say, heart pounding as I wrap my arms around his neck.

"What do you get, beautiful?"

"Not knowing what comes next is part of the fun," I say as he sets me on my feet. "The uncertainty and being just a little bit scared—it makes everything so much more intense."

"And this was just a corn maze." He unties my blindfold, easing it away from my eyes as he adds in a softer voice, "Imagine how much fun other things could be with this kind of trust."

I blink, eyes prickling as they adjust to the dim light of dusk, and Will's face slowly comes into focus. He's so close and he smells so good—clean and Will-ish and beautifully familiar—that I suddenly can't help myself. I press up on tiptoe, bringing my mouth to his for our first kiss in way too long.

And just like the first time I kissed Will, back when I was eighteen years old and had no idea what it was like to kiss a grown man who knew what he wanted and wasn't afraid to show how much he wanted it, sparks fly, the earth spins faster, and my universe is rearranged.

Back then, it was love at first sight. Now, it's confirmation that the chemistry between us is every bit as combustible as it was before, that it might even be a little bit wilder, and a little bit sweeter, after our experiment here tonight.

"Sorry," I whisper when we finally pull apart. "I couldn't help myself."

"Why are you apologizing?" he asks, his hands gliding down to squeeze my ass through my jeans.

"You're supposed to be in charge."

"That doesn't mean you can't kiss me whenever you want," he says with a wink. "Assuming I don't have you tied up in a position that makes kissing difficult."

I grin, the thought not nearly as intimidating as it used to be. "Oh. Okay. That's good to know, sir."

"All done with sir. For now." He smoothes my hair away from my face, holding it in place as the breeze does its best to undo his tidying work. "You did a good job. A great job."

"Thanks." I wrap my arms around his waist, feeling closer to him than I have in a long time. And feeling hopeful, too. So hopeful I can't help asking, "Does this mean I'm ready to graduate to Lesson Two?"

He shakes his head in mock disapproval. "Always in such a rush."

"Can't blame me for being an eager pupil when I have such a good teacher." I press closer to him, biting my bottom lip as my belly brushes against clear evidence that I'm not the only one affected by that kiss.

His eyes darken in response, and when he speaks, there isn't a hint of humor in his words. "I brought you here for a reason, Hailey. Because I'm not sure I can be trusted in a room alone with you."

"You can always be trusted," I whisper, tipping my head back, bringing my mouth closer to his. "And we agreed that these lessons were going to be hands on..." I brush my hot lips against his hotter ones as I add in a temptress voice I barely recognize, "So why shouldn't you get your hands on me, sir? Preferably all over me. Everywhere."

My next breath ends in a groan as his mouth covers mine in a kiss that isn't the slightest bit sweet. This kiss stakes a claim, makes demands, and issues a warning—back away now or prepare to be taken in ways I may never have been taken before. But I'm not scared or even intimidated. I'm turned on, fired up, and ready for everything this no-holds-barred version of Will wants to share with me.

"My place," I pant against his lips when we finally come up for air. "It's closer. And we can get our clothes off faster."

"Race you to the truck," he says, and then we're both off, dashing back through the maze as the first stars begin to wink on in the clear blue sky.

CHAPTER 10

WILL

*T*wenty minutes—and several violations of state speed laws—later, we stumble into Hailey's apartment, mouths fused and hands everywhere. After only a few feet, I lose patience with the pace of our progress toward the bedroom and reach down, hooking my hands behind Hailey's knees and urging them around my waist. She moans her approval against my lips, locking her legs tight above my hips as I palm her bottom in my hands and make haste toward her bedroom. "I'm still on the pill and clean," she gasps against my lips.

"Me, too," I echo. "The clean part."

She smiles against my lips, and I kiss her deeper, moaning as I squeeze her sweet ass tight, pinning her against my rock-hard length as I move.

I had a game plan for tonight, one that didn't involve so much as a kiss, let alone carrying Hailey straight to bed—do not pass go, do not discuss her safe word in further detail—but now I realize how naïve it was to think I could plan this like any other scene.

This isn't any other scene, and Hailey isn't any other sub. She's the woman I love, the woman I haven't been able to stop thinking about, dreaming about, for months. I've jerked off to memories of being buried inside her more times than I can count, each release ending with a sharp wave of pain rushing in fast behind the pleasure as reality came crashing in, reminding me that I was never going to have Hailey in my bed again.

But here she is, stretching out in front of me on top of her pale blue and green quilt, her skin golden in the glow from the exposed bulbs strung across the ceiling. The lighting makes her bed look like a table at a trendy restaurant, and I intend to make the most of scoring this oh-so-coveted seat.

I note the slats in her headboard and don't hesitate to order, "Arms over your head, wrists crossed."

"Yes, sir." Hailey lifts her arms without missing a beat, her eager obedience making my cock pulse against my fly. I'm desperate to be out of my clothes and skin-to-skin with her, but I'm determined to take this slow. I want to drive Hailey crazy, make her beg for me before I grant her the relief we're both so desperate for. I want to give her a taste of what obedience and delayed satisfaction can do for her if she willing to put herself in my hands.

"Your safe word is ninja," I remind her. "Do you still have those scarves you used to wear as belts a few years ago?"

"The silk ones?" She nods. "Yes, sir. In my closet. On the hooks to the right."

"Perfect." I fetch a silk scarf from the collection in Hailey's closet and cross back to the bed, holding her hooded gaze as I deftly bind her wrists to each other before securing them to the headboard. "If you want me to stop or unbind you, you use your safe word, not 'no' or 'stop.' Do you understand?"

"Why?" she asks in a soft voice, her eyes going wide.

"Because sometimes 'no' and 'stop' are part of the game, Curious," I say, reaching for the top button on her blouse and slowing slipping it through the hole. "You might find yourself screaming 'no' when you really mean 'yes' or 'stop' when you really mean 'go.'" I open another button, balls growing heavier as the white lace of her bra comes into view. "When we agree to suspend the usual rules, it opens the door to different kinds of play and for words to have multiple meanings."

"All right, sir," she says, teeth digging into her kiss-swollen bottom lip as I finish unbuttoning her shirt and part the fabric, revealing her taut stomach and the tight nipples pressing against the lace of her bra. "But I'm not sure I'm going to be into that kind of play. I like no to mean no."

"Understandable, and there's no pressure to do anything that doesn't feel right. You will always be able to put on the brakes, whenever you want. But when we're together like this ninja is your 'no,' Hailey. Do you understand?"

She nods, shivering as I mold my hands to her ribs

beneath her breasts, relishing the bliss of being able to touch her like this again. Like she's mine.

"Cold?" I ask, voice husky.

She shakes her head and whispers, "No again, sir."

"Scared?" I slide my thumbs beneath her bra, teasing back and forth across the sinfully soft skin on the underside of her breasts.

She shakes her head again.

"Then what are you feeling, Cat? Tell me how you feel."

"Excited. Electric," she says, adding in a husky voice that slays me, "Like I can't wait for you to touch me."

"Touch you where?"

"Everywhere." She sighs as I bend, pressing a kiss to her chest, right above her pounding heart. "Please, Will, touch me everywhere."

Her words snap something inside of me, severing the tether on the control I usually take for granted when I'm calling the shots in the bedroom, and before I've made the conscious decision to take things to the next level, I've shoved her bra under her armpits, baring her sweet, perfect tits. This is what she does to me, this woman. She drives me crazy, which is going to make topping her even more of a challenge, more of a pleasure.

I make love to her breasts with my mouth, circling each tight nipple with my tongue, dragging my teeth across the sensitive underside of her fullness, sucking and biting until she's squirming beneath me, panting as she writhes against her bonds.

"Oh God, please." She loops one leg around my

waist, using her considerable strength to attempt to pull me closer. "Please, sir, I want you so much."

"All things in good time, baby," I promise, holding strong and holding back, making sure no part of me touches the needy place between her thighs. "But first, a brief refresher course on what we learned tonight. Lie flat on the bed and close your eyes."

After the briefest hesitation, her lashes flutter closed, and her shapely leg lengthens back onto the increasingly rumpled quilt.

As soon as she's still, I sit back between her spread legs, admiring how beautiful she looks with her shirt open, her breasts swollen from my mouth, and her arms bound over her head. "Now I want you to tell me, how close are you to disobeying an order? On a scale from one to five, one being not at all tempted to disobey and five being ready to rumble for what you want."

"A one." Her back arching, she adds, "I feel like I'm on fire with wanting you, but I don't want to break the rules."

"Good." I reach down, tracing my fingers slowly down between her breasts with their tightly puckered tips. "And why don't you want to break the rules?"

"Because I trust you."

"Is that all?" I circle her navel, feeling the pulse of her heart beneath my fingertips as her belly flutters.

"And because I like it," she whispers, trapping her bottom lip between her teeth in a way that makes me crazy. "I like doing what I'm told, not having to make any of the decisions, just doing what you tell me to do. It makes me…"

"It makes you what, baby? Tell me."

"It makes me wet. So wet," she says, sending a fresh rush of desire rocketing through my body until it screams for me to strip off her jeans and find out just how wet my girl is. For me to spread her thighs wide and sink deep into her slick heat and fuck her with all the passion I've been keeping bottled up tight for so long.

Instead, I grit my jaw and force my touch to remain whisper-soft as I return my attention to her nipples, circling her tight tips with my thumbs. "I love making you wet, sweetheart, but I don't just want you wet tonight. I want you dripping. By the time I get you down to your panties I want them to be soaking wet. Do you understand?"

She whimpers softly, her throat working as she nods. "Yes, sir."

"And so I want to try something different. You can open your eyes." I wait for her lashes to sweep up and her lust-fogged gaze to focus before I reach into my front pocket, pulling out the silver buds I brought to share with her and holding them up to the light. "I was going to leave these here as a gift for you when I left tonight. I wanted to give you time to look them over, try them on, see what you thought about adding them into our lesson plan. But now that I have you here, naked and at my mercy, I don't want to wait. Do you know what these are?"

Heat flickers in her eyes. "Nipple clamps?"

I nod. "Have you ever played with clamps before?" I ask, fighting to keep my voice calm and even. I know there's an excellent chance that Hailey's slept with someone else in the past year, but I can't afford to let ex-boyfriend Will get code-red, stab-a-fucker jealous about that. As her instructor in the art of pleasure and pain, I need to know if she understands what to expect as I tighten the clamps—that's all.

But I would be lying if I didn't admit that I'm relieved as hell when she shakes her head. "No, but I've read about them. And I was...curious."

"Curious Cat," I murmur as I roll one of her nipples between my fingers and thumb. "Are you curious enough to skip ahead a few lessons tonight?"

She nods again, her lips parting on a gasp as I pinch her nipple tight.

"Just remember, if this gets too intense, you have your safe word."

"I'm not afraid," she says. Defiance sparks in her eyes, making my blood pump even faster, hotter.

"Famous last words, baby." I lean down, capturing her swollen tip in my mouth, sucking her hard and deep. Her sigh turns to a groan as she arches closer, whimpering as I tease her sensitive flesh between my teeth. I wait until her hips are lifting off the bed, seeking relief, before I bring the first clamp to her slick flesh and trap her nipple between the textured rubber pads. "Hips down and lie still," I order, tightening the clamp as I rock my thigh between hers, grinding against her clit.

A sound of relief bursts from deep in her chest, only to become a growl of frustration as I put an end to the friction. My lips curve as I shift onto the mattress on her left side and press a gentle kiss to her unadorned nipple. I can't wait to introduce her to the sweet torture of delayed gratification, to teach her how swiftly relief can become pain and pain can become unimaginable pleasure.

I agreed to teach Hailey because I couldn't stomach the idea of another man's hands on her. I never imagined it would be this insanely satisfying to guide her first steps into the dark garden. But she's a natural, taking to submission like she was born to blossom under a Dominant's care.

I'm simultaneously thrilled and enraged that I never dared to take her in hand like this before.

How could I have missed the signs? How could I have so vastly underestimated her strength, passion, and imagination? How in God's name did I get here—teaching the woman I love how to submit for another man?

The thought sends a wave of regret through me so strong I can't keep the words filling my head from my lips. "I wish it was me, Curious. I wish I was the man you're so eager to please." I lift my head, catching her gaze in the dim light, surprised to see tears shining in her eyes.

"Of course it's you," she whispers, making my heart skip a beat. "I heard you on the roof," she continues, her breath hitching as she adds, "Last September, when you were talking to that man. Sterling. I heard you telling him about our vanilla sex life and all the rest of it, and I just...fell apart. I felt like I would never be enough for you."

My eyebrows shoot up, but after a moment of consideration, it all clicks into place. This is the missing piece, the part of the story I couldn't make sense of before. This is why Hailey pushed me away.

And this is why she went looking for a teacher—because she wants to try to make this work, make *us* work.

Because she wants me back as much as I want her.

The knowledge melts the walls around my heart so fast it's all I can do not to kiss her senseless. To surge over her, spread her legs, and glide inside her right this fucking second. I need to be with her again, to show her how much I love her, to prove to her with every thrust into her sweetness that she has always been and *will* always be everything I want and everything I need.

But in this moment, I'm still Will the teacher, and I have a responsibility to my student to hold the safe space she was promised when I first tied her to this bed.

"Thank you for telling me." I press a soft kiss to the curve of her beautiful breast. "I can't wait to talk more about this, but first we're going to finish the lesson. Unless you need to use your safe word?"

She blinks faster, clearly confused, but after a moment she shakes her head. "No, sir, I don't need to use my safe word."

"Good." I roll her nipple between my fingers, making her gasp as I slip the second clamp into place. "And what about these lessons?" I ask as I attach the chain in my other pocket to first one clamp and then the other, watching Hailey watch me with hooded eyes. "Are you still curious, Curious?"

This time she doesn't hesitate before nodding. "Yes, sir. I'm still curious. I'm especially curious about what that chain is for."

"It's for this, sweetheart." I give the chain a gentle pull, tugging on her bound nipples the barest bit, but the effect is everything I hoped for and more.

Hailey gasps, her body bowing off the bed. When I release the pressure, she sags back onto the mattress with a moan that's music to my ears.

"You like that?" I whisper in her ear, cock swelling even harder, thicker as she whispers, "Yes, sir. So much, sir."

"Then I think you'll like what comes next." I reach down, popping the button at the top of her jeans, loving the way she shivers beneath me as I drag her jeans down her legs. Her panties come next, and then I'm between her legs, spreading her strong, silky soft thighs and settling in to worship the sweet pussy I've missed so fucking much.

To worship, and also to torture, because that's what I'm here for. To teach her about pleasure and pain and the way they can bleed into each other to make her come so hard she'll never forget this lesson, this moment, or who was between her legs when she learned the things a Dominant man can make her feel. I don't know where Hailey and I go from here, but I know that I want to rock her world.

I start slowly, pressing a kiss to one thigh and then the other before guiding her legs wider, wider, until she's completely exposed to me and every slick fold of her wet pussy is mine to admire, to devour.

"Beautiful," I murmur before teasing my tongue up one side of her swollen sex and down the other, carefully avoiding her clit as I get her hotter, wetter. I wait until her hips are urgently lifting toward my mouth, seeking a more intimate connection before I bring one hand to her entrance and capture the chain with the other.

Then, at the moment I tug the chain, I push two fingers into her heat, penetrating her to my first knuckle. The sound she makes—part gasp, part groan, and all feverishly aroused woman—is enough to make my dick throb painfully between my legs, but I don't rush. I tug again and thrust deeper, tug and thrust, tug and thrust, introducing my gorgeous girl to the world of pleasure-pain while she continues to make sexy, turned-on sounds that assure me she's loving every minute of what I'm doing to her body.

Her pussy tells me, too.

She's so wet, so hot. It isn't long before my fingers are dripping with her juices and the salty-sweet smell of her arousal is swirling through my head and I'm fighting a losing battle with my own self-control.

I want to be inside her so desperately I'm about to shatter a molar, but I need her to come first. I drive my fingers deeper, adding a third when Hailey bucks into my hand, silently begging me to move faster. So I do, fucking her hard and fast with my hand as I hold the chain tight, applying constant pressure to her bound nipples.

She cries out in pain, but only a second later, the sound becomes a shout of triumph as she tumbles over, coming so hard I can feel her inner walls convulsing around my fingers. And it is as hot as any fantasy I've ever had of Hailey under my control—hotter, because *she's* hotter, wilder, abandoning herself to the experience with a bravery that brings me to my knees.

"Oh God, Will. Oh God, please, inside me," she begs as the waves begin to abate. "Oh please, inside me, please."

"Please, sir," I remind her in a rough voice, but I'm already tugging at my belt and ripping open my pants. A second later I'm over her, my lips fused to hers as I gently detach the clamps. I catch her cries of pleasure-pain in my mouth, swallowing them as I swirl my tongue against hers.

The moment I come up for air, she gasps, "Please, sir. Please."

And because I can deny her nothing, not when she's like this, I shove my jeans and boxers down around my thighs and position myself at her entrance. And even though I'm so desperate to be inside her that my hand is shaking and my heart is thundering in my ears, I pause for a beat.

Another.

And then just one more.

Because I want to remember. I want to tattoo the way it feels to glide inside her on my memory, to bottle up this moment I wasn't sure would ever come again so I can drink deep from it on nights when she's far away from me and all I want is her. All I want is this. All I want is her taste in my mouth and her body hot and eager against mine and her sweet voice calling out my name as I push oh so deep, so fucking deep.

"Yes, oh, yes," she cries out, arching beneath me, taking me even deeper.

And then there is nothing but her heat and her fire and the way she takes me to all the places I want to be, to something sweeter than paradise because it belongs only to Hailey and me. To us together. It is a place we created with love and five years of devotion to bringing each other pleasure.

But this time is special. Sharper, edgier, but still overflowing with emotion, and by the time she comes a second time, I can't stop myself from following her over. I come hard, my balls clutching between my legs as I empty myself into her pulsing heat.

After, once I've finally caught my breath, I push myself up on my forearms, loosening the scarf binding her wrists.

"Thank you, sir," Hailey says, rolling her hands in circles.

"Of course, Curious," I say, gazing down into her flushed face as I add, "Ninja," in a softer voice.

Her lashes flutter, and her lips curve in a lazy smile. "I thought that was my safe word."

"It is, but I need to borrow it. I need to talk to Hailey my ex, not Hailey my student," I say, pushing on when she nods. "I'm sorry. I hate that you overheard something that made you feel like you weren't enough for me. You're more than enough, and you always have been. I always felt honored and privileged to be the man in your bed, baby, no matter what we did or didn't do together."

Hailey swallows, and her tongue slips out to dampen her lips, but she doesn't say a word, not a word, for so long I feel compelled to add, "But you were perfect tonight. A natural. And I'm happy to keep teaching you if that's what you want."

"I want," she says with a surety that goes straight to my cock. "The fact that you were the one who answered my ad, it just seems…meant to be. And I really want to know, Will. If I can be what you want me to be. And if I can't…" She glances away, severing the intimate eye contact. "Well, I want to know that, too."

I want to tell her that all I want is her—fuck the lessons, fuck everything but her and me and how perfect it is to be back in bed with her—but I can tell that she's serious. She truly wants to test her boundaries, to open her mind, to see if we can work this way as well as we did in all the other ways.

So I press a kiss to her forehead and promise, "Then I will be the very best teacher I can be."

And I mean it, even though it's going to be hard as hell not to fall back into loving her so fiercely that I can't tell where she ends and I begin, so deeply that it will feel like a vital organ is being ripped out of me if she decides submission isn't for her, after all.

But if that happens, I'll just have to convince her that we don't need the game. That all we need is each other.

It's true. Right now, with her gaze locked on mine and her fingers skimming up and down my back as my cock thickens inside her, I lack for nothing.

Though, I can't deny I enjoyed our first lesson. Enjoyed it a hell of a lot.

"Ready for a chance to earn some bonus points for lesson one?" I ask, arching a teasing brow.

She smiles that beautiful, fearless grin that won my heart on our very first date, when she swore to try any sushi roll I had the guts to order, even the one that was served still squirming on the plate.

"Then let me teach you what these clamps can do to your pussy, Miss Marks," I murmur, laughing as her eyes go wide. "Don't worry," I assure her. "I'll be gentle. At least at first…"

"Well, that's reassuring, sir," she says, slipping back into the game with an ease that makes me hope this is only the first night of many.

And that these aren't just lessons, but a new beginning for me and this woman I love beyond all measure.

CHAPTER 11

HAILEY

For the first time in so long, I don't dream.

Ever since I was a little kid, I've had action movie dreams, filled with so much drama and suspense that I often wake up exhausted, feeling like I've hardly slept at all. A hard workout during the day usually helps to quiet my night brain, but even that doesn't always get the job done, and sex almost always has the opposite effect. Instead of calming me down, it shifts my dreams into overdrive.

After an especially steamy evening, I can usually count on waking up at least twice, soaked in sweat after barely escaping motorcycle-riding velociraptors or fire-breathing flying monkeys or whatever else my over-stimulated brain has brewed up with the influx of pleasure hormones.

But this morning when I slit my eyes, taking in the pale light prickling through my yellow curtains, for a moment I can't believe it's morning. Without dreams to mark the passage of time, or even a midnight trip to the bathroom, I feel disoriented.

What happened between the moment I passed out on Will's chest and this moment? Where was I if not in dreamland?

I have no clue, but after a moment I decide this is the kind of weirdness I could get used to.

Who cares where I was or what my brain was up to? If I could wake up feeling this relaxed and refreshed every morning, I would consider myself a lucky girl.

You should arrange for Will to tie you up and make you scream every night.

The thought makes me blush then grin so wide my cheeks start to cramp. I roll over, burying my burning face in my pillow as memories of all the wicked things Will did to me last night come rushing back.

In the light of day, it's a little embarrassing, but I wouldn't take back a second of what we shared. At least, not the experimenting part...

I do wish I'd been able to keep the truth from Will a little longer—for his own protection—but by the time I started making those confessions, I wasn't thinking with my rational mind. Letting Will take the lead wasn't just sexy as hell, it also did a number on my self-defense system. All those walls I've worked so hard to keep in place since we separated came tumbling down so fast it made my head spin.

And I'm sure the nipple clamps didn't help things any.

Nipple clamps. I let my lover put clamps on my nipples and other, even more intimate places last night.

Who is this wild, experimental person, and where has level-headed Hailey gone?

"Good morning, Curious," Will says from the door to my bedroom. "You ready for breakfast?"

I roll over, the goofy grin rushing back to my face as I meet his dancing eyes. He looks as giddy as I feel, which for some reason makes me giggle.

"What's so funny?" he asks with a smile.

"Nothing. Everything." I lift my hand to cover my mouth and add in a stage whisper, "We did naughty things in this bed last night, William Major Saunders."

He chuckles. "We did, Hailey Rae Marks. So how are you feeling about that now that morning has broken?"

I prop up against the pillows as I thread my fingers together in my lap. "I'm feeling good," I say, my toes squirming beneath the covers as I meet Will's searching gaze and start blushing all over again. "Great, actually. I slept like a rock. Best sleep I've had in forever."

"Glad to hear it." He steps into the room, carrying a tray mounded with a plate of pastries, a bowl of fresh fruit and yogurt, and a French press filled with coffee. "Hopefully you woke up hungry, too."

I press my lips together, shaking my head as Will settles the tray across my lap. "You didn't have to do this. We could have eaten together at the table."

"I know I didn't have to." He leans down, bringing his face level with mine. "I wanted to. I wanted to do something to show you how grateful I am for last night. And for you. And for your honesty."

I bring a hand to his face, cupping his stubbly cheek. "You don't have to thank me. It was wonderful. And it probably could have been wonderful a lot sooner if I'd been honest with you instead of running away."

"I understand why you ran," he says, leaning into my touch. "It's a big thing to keep secret, and I never should have discussed the intimate details of our relationship with someone else. I should have told Sterling that I appreciated his concern, but that our sex life was between you and me and no one else."

"We both could have handled things better," I agree, anxiety spiking again as I brush his hair from his forehead. "But I want you to promise me that you'll be honest with me from now on, even if it's hard. And I'll do the same."

He turns his head, pressing a kiss to my palm. "Done. Honesty, even if it hurts."

"And no holding back," I add in a softer voice. "I need to know if this will really work, and that can't happen if you're giving me the PG-13 version of what you want. You get what I'm saying?"

His lips curve. "I get it, but we're only three days in, woman. It's okay to take things slow. You need to learn how to walk before I ask you to run." He presses a kiss to my forehead that makes me warm all over. "No one ever made it from the couch to a 5k by sprinting the entire distance the first day of training, right?"

"I see your point." I scoot over, moving the tray with me, and pat the mattress. "Sit down and stay a while? There's more than enough to share."

He straightens, taking a step away from the bed. "I would love to, but I was doing some thinking this morning while I was out getting pastries."

"That sounds ominous…"

Will smiles. "Not ominous at all. I just don't think it's a good idea for us to fall back into old habits. At least, not some of them."

My brow furrows. "What do you mean?"

"I mean sex and intimacy outside the game," he says, sending heat rushing to my cheeks again. "Right now, all I want to do is crawl into bed with you, feed you breakfast, lick honey off your nipples, and make love to you slow and sweet until lunch time."

My lashes flutter. "Sounds like a solid plan to me. I've missed that part of us."

"I have, too," he says softly. "But if we start down that road, I'm going to lose all objectivity and the distance I need to be a good teacher. And I'd probably lose what's left of my self-preservation instinct, too." He runs a hand through his hair with a sad smile. "Until we know for sure that this second chance is a go, I can't get too attached to the idea of you and me together again, Hailey. Losing you was…so hard. Crazy fucking hard, and I don't want to go through that kind of grief again unless I absolutely have to."

Chest aching, I hold his gaze, hoping he can see how truly sorry I am to have brought him pain. "I know it was hard. It was hard for me, too. That's why I tried to keep the lie about the other man going. I didn't want to get your hopes up and let you down if I can't be the person you need me to be. I didn't want to risk hurting you again like that. I—" I'm about to say 'I love you,' but I bite back the words at the last minute, replacing them with, "I care about you."

He's right; we have to take this slow and do our best not to fall thoughtlessly back into old habits. I do love Will—I will always love him—but saying the words aloud infers a level of commitment I'm not prepared to make just yet. For me, love is a promise that's backed up with actions. So, until I'm prepared to walk the walk, I should avoid talking the talk.

"You're not going to let me down," Will says. "And I don't want you to worry about hurting me, okay? I'm a big boy, and I can take care of myself. The only thing you should be concerned about is being honest and open and enjoying yourself as we experiment. And as soon as these lessons stop being fun, you let me know."

I nod seriously. "I will. I promise."

"Perfect. We'll worry about the other stuff after your graduation ceremony," he says with a wiggle of his eyebrows. "Which I should probably start shopping for. At this rate, you're going to be graduating early, and I want to make sure you're dressed appropriately for the occasion."

Forcing a lighter tone, I quip, "Something leather with spiky studs, I'm hoping?"

"Something like that," he says, winking as he backs toward the door. "Enjoy your breakfast, beautiful. I'll see you Monday night."

My lips turn down, and disappointment rushes through my chest. "What about tonight? You don't have a game, right?"

"Tonight is a night off to rest, relax, and process." He pauses in the doorway, looking so delicious in the morning light it's almost physically painful to look at him. "Like I said, we're walking before we run. You need time off in between scenes or you risk losing perspective."

"All right," I say, though I'm pretty sure I'm already losing perspective, since seeing Will about to walk out of my bedroom makes me feel like it's raining frogs on my wedding day. "Then I'll see you Monday."

"Monday," he repeats. "I'll text you with the details later. Goodbye, Curious." He turns to go, but at the last second leans back into the room to add, "So far you're getting an A-plus in this course, by the way."

I roll my eyes, but I'm grinning as I say, "Good to know. I would like extra sparkle stickers on my report card, please."

"Done," he says with a laugh. "Have a great day."

"You, too. And thank you for breakfast," I say, pouring a cup of coffee as he vanishes from my doorway.

But I'm not focusing on the rich, steamy brown liquid flowing into my cup. I'm counting Will's steps as he crosses the apartment, my heart sinking deeper and deeper into a sad pit as I hear the front door open and close.

He's gone. And I won't see him again until Monday.

The knowledge is truly crushing.

Since we ended things last year, I've gone far longer than a day without seeing Will—as long as a couple weeks once we smoothed out our communication system for gym business and he stopped frequenting my favorite coffee shop. And though I never stopped missing him, I learned how to get by and stay positive.

I'm an independent woman who understands that I'm ultimately responsible for my own happiness, no matter how hurt I might be by the secrets my boyfriend kept from me or anything else the people in my life might do to let me down.

But I've clearly underestimated how deeply jumping back into bed with Will would affect me. Especially this kind of jumping, the kind that involves shutting down my own self-defense system and trusting in Will to keep me safe.

I don't regret last night for a second—it was insanely fun and sexy and oh-so-satisfying in every way—but Will is probably right. A day off to process might keep me from getting in too deep too fast.

I pour cream into my coffee and swirl the spoon, mentally scrolling through my stay-on-track strategies, the habits I turn to when I'm feeling down and out. Since Will and I split, when loneliness threatened to suck me down into the misery hole, I've found solace in work, exercise, friends, and family.

But the gym is closed on Sundays, my parents are on a European tour, and I already had my fun Saturday with Sabrina yesterday. She'll be at work all day, pulling a double in an effort to make rent. I could go by her bar and visit, but she would inevitably ask me how Lesson One went, and what can I really say about that except "good"?

The private details are too private for sister dish-time, and I don't really *want* to share them, anyway. I want to keep them just between Will and me.

Which leaves exercise as my sole recourse for mood

elevation. So even though I'm not at all in the mood for a run, I finish my breakfast, change into my gear, and hit the pavement. I run my usual three and a half miles —the perfect training for the 5k races I've got lined up this fall—and then decide to keep going. I'm not tired, and my thoughts are still a ball of knotted yarn rolling around in my head. I haven't gotten close to untangling them or sorting out what I'm feeling aside from "missing Will and wishing he had never left."

I push through my usual mile-seven energy dip and loop around for another trip through downtown, taking my total distance to eight or nine miles before I slow to a walk for my cooldown. I'm still restless, but if I run any farther, I'll regret it tomorrow when I have to spend the entire day teaching my advanced students how to take assailants twice their size to the mat.

And so I slip into Cathedral Juicery for a post-run lemonade and move on to stage two of my Get Grounded plan. Borrowing a pen from the juice barista, I snag a couple of napkins and sit down at a sunny side-walk table to make a Pro and Con list. It's a little cool, and most of the people around me are wearing jackets, but my skin is still giving off heat from my run, making me grateful for the breeze blowing off the Willamette River.

There won't be many more perfect Sunday mornings like this. Soon, autumn will truly take hold and we won't see temperatures in the seventies until next June. The thought makes me melancholy—I love Portland, but the rainy winters can be a bummer—and the first item on my list ends up being a Con.

Con one: Staying away from Will until Monday means no hugs for at least forty-eight hours. Or at least no Will hugs, which are the best hugs.

How could I have let him leave this morning without getting a goodbye hug? I've been suffering from Will hug withdrawal for months and not rushing in shouldn't mean that a friendly embrace is off-limits.

I make a mental note to ask Will if hugs are approved teacher-student interactions and add a pro to my list:

Pro one: By staying away from Will until Monday I will be following directions like a good student, proving to both Will and myself that I've got submissive potential.

Almost immediately, however, I add four more cons.

Con two: If I pretend I'm fine with waiting until Monday, I will be lying to both Will and myself. I don't want to wait until Monday. I want to see him now.

Con three: If I go home and spend the afternoon alone, I'll be too distracted to focus on anything productive and end up wasting an entire afternoon binge watching Gilmore Girls for the tenth time and eating an entire pizza by myself.

Con four: And if I eat an entire pizza by myself, I won't sleep well tonight, and I'll be wasted for work tomorrow.

Con five: And if I'm wasted for work tomorrow, someone could get hurt, and even if no one gets hurt, I'll be too tired to follow directions like a good submissive on Monday, and we'll have to reschedule Lesson Two anyway, so we should just go ahead and reschedule it now—for tonight.

Scrunching up my nose, I valiantly fight to whip up another item for the Pro list, but I come up empty. Looking at the list, it's a no-brainer. The safety of innocent students practically depends on me going over to Will's.

Okay, so that's a bit of a stretch, but surely Will can find it in his heart to forgive me for disobeying an order, once I make it clear to him that his delay of Lesson Two was short-sighted.

Especially if I provide a suitable distraction to keep him from getting too worked up about my teeny-tiny violation of the power exchange class terms of service...

And I have the perfect distraction in mind.

With a grin, I stuff my list into the side pocket of my leggings, leave my empty juice glass in the dirty dish bin, and hit the pavement at a jog. I've already run over twice my usual distance today, but I'm suddenly filled with energy and in too much of a hurry for a leisurely stroll.

The sooner I get home, the sooner I can shower and head for the condo Will and I shared for years, the space that still pops up in my head when I think of home.

CHAPTER 12

**From the texts of Will Saunders and
Shane Wallace**

Shane Wallace: You told Sabrina I was the rat! How
could you, man? I was trying to keep a low profile
with her.

Will Saunders: I didn't tell her. I didn't say a word about
you when we talked.

Shane: Well, she figured it out somehow. Some buddies
and I ended up at her bar on a pub crawl last night, and
she gave me no end of shit about being a tattletale who
reports back to Big Brother.

Will: LOL. Well, you are kind of a tattletale.

Shane: I was trying to spare the girl an STD and a broken heart! I was trying to be a gentleman. But if this is the kind of treatment I get for doing the right thing, next time, I'll keep my mouth shut.

Will: I was just kidding, Walls. Of course I'm glad you said something. I don't want her to get hooked up with a douchebag. But like my biological little sisters, Sabrina's also stubborn as hell and is going to do what she pleases, no matter what Big Brother has to say about it.
At least you tried to spare her the pain of driving her car off the edge of the heartbreak cliff.

Shane: Why doesn't that make me feel any better?

Will: I don't know. Maybe you're feeling lousy because your warning wasn't purely altruistic?

Shane: Maybe I'm feeling lousy because you use big words and it's annoying. I have a junior college degree in welding, asshole. Adjust your vocab.

Will: I will not. You're a smart kid, Wallace. You'd be even smarter if you spent more time reading and less time drinking beer.

Shane: But I like beer, and I need to drink it while I'm still young enough to drink all weekend and still kick ass at practice on Monday. And yeah, I guess I'm smart enough, but I'm tired today. So can you just say what you're saying?

Will: I'm saying that you have a thing for Sabrina and that's the real reason you don't want her dating this guy. Because he's nice looking and plays a good game and will actually give you a run for your money when you finally decide to man up and ask her out.

Shane: That's not true! That's not even close to being true! I don't want to date Sabrina. She's a complete pain in the ass.

Will: Oh man, you really like her, don't you? You've got it bad.

Shane: Like her? Yeah, right. I like her like I like burning my tongue on hot pizza and not being able to taste anything for three days. I like her like I like multiple paper cuts on my fingers on a day I'm making lemonade. I like her like I like getting a puck to the nuts and realizing I forgot to put on my cup before the game.

Will: I think thou dost protest too much.

Shane: And I think thou dost have your head up your own ass. I don't like the girl. And even if I did think she was worth the hassle and possible hearing loss associated with dating someone who NEVER STOPS TALKING, she's off-limits. No dating team members' siblings, remember?

Will: She's not a team member's sibling. She's my ex-girlfriend's little sister. Even if Hailey and I were to get back together for the long haul, the rules don't apply to in-laws.

Shane: Really? You're serious?

Will: I'm serious. Though I would, of course, absolutely kick your face through your asshole if you hurt Bree in any way. But I happen to think you're a fairly decent guy, all things considered.

Shane: All things considered? What's that supposed to mean? I'm not the one who laughs like a howler monkey every time Cruise pranks Nowicki.

Will: I regret nothing. Cruise is a master of his craft, and laughter is good for the soul.

Shane: True. He is a diabolical son of a bitch.
So, on a serious note, were you for real about you and Hailey getting back together? Has there been activity on that front I'm not aware of? I thought it was hardcore over between you two.

Will: Yeah, so did I.
But there have been some...developments.
Nothing I'm at liberty to discuss, but we cleared the air, discovered our break-up could be chalked up to poor

communication on both sides, and agreed to work on some things that might make us a stronger couple. I think there's a chance we'll be able to make it work. I'm trying not to get my hopes up too high, but…yeah. Definitely a chance.

Shane: Good. I'm happy for you, man. I always thought you and Hailey were great together. Seeing you two break up shook my faith in coupledom.

Will: Me, too.

Shane: Yeah. I figured if you two couldn't make it, I'm probably fucked before I get started. Even if I do find someone willing to put up with my crazy travel schedule and my collection of salt and pepper shakers.

Will: How many are you up to now?

Shane: About fifty. Hit a junk shop in St. Helens last week and scored two creepy as fuck bunnies with glowing red eyes, and a set from the 1930s with baby heads on chicken bodies. Seriously disturbing stuff.

Will: Keep it up and you'll beat out Cruise for weirdest hobby.

Shane: It's not weird; it's research. The salt and pepper shakers are just a side project, something to hunt for while I'm out scoping out different business models. I'm thinking of opening up an antique store when I retire. I like old stuff and giving forgotten treasures a new lease on life.

Will: Why wait until you retire? Hailey and I bought the gym when I was only a few years into my contract, and the business has grown every year since. By the time I hang up my skates, I'll have a steady income stream to help ease the transition as I figure out my next incarnation.

Shane: I like that. Incarnation. It makes retiring sound like something exciting instead of terrifying. Speaking of terrifying, did you hear Brendan after the game on Friday? He said he's thinking this might be his last season.

Will: He's been saying that for the past three years.

Shane: I think this time is different. Apparently he got an offer to go coach for the expansion team in Kansas City.

Will: No way. He hates those lame-ass fucks as much as the rest of us. How can he even think about teaching them all our secrets? Not that it will help. They have as much fire on the ice as day-old dog shit.

Shane: I don't know. Maybe he's just old and tired?

Will: Maybe…

Hell.

Makes you think.

Shane: It does. I'm already twenty-five. I can't believe the time has gone by so fast.

Will: Cry me a river, kid. I'm staring down the barrel of thirty-two.

Shane: So if Brendan and Petrov both quit, you and Cruise will be the new old fogies, huh? That just seems wrong. I like to be able to look up to my team captain…

Will: I'm not too old to drive over there and teach you some manners, asshole.

Shane: LOL. I'm kidding, man. I mean, Cruise is a clown, and you've got that weird laugh sometimes, but either one of you would be a great captain. It just makes you think, you know, about how time isn't standing still.

Will: No, it's not.

Shane: Maybe I will start looking into a business loan sooner rather than later. I've already got a lot of solid ideas on how to make my shop stand out in the crowd around here.

Will: Go for it. Let me know if you need help with your business plan. I've got a great guy. And if you decide to ask Sabrina out, make sure to mind your manners. If I hear you've been anything but a gentleman, I won't be happy, and neither will you.

Shane: Understood. And good luck with Hailey. I'll be rooting for both of you.

CHAPTER 13

WILL

*S*hane's words haunt me the rest of the day.

He's right—time isn't standing still. And though I know my first call was the right one, and that Hailey needs time to process what happened between us last night, I can't help regretting the decision to put off lesson two until tomorrow.

I don't want to wait.

I don't want to waste a single second alone that could be spent with the woman I love.

Being with her again after so long apart was so emotionally intense I woke up feeling like I'd just played pond hockey all day in sub-zero temperatures, but I don't want a break. I want to keep skating, headed straight for the thin ice at the center of the lake, and if I fall through and drown in the frigid waters, at least I'll go out in the arms of my favorite person in the world.

She truly is my favorite. She's my home base, my safe space, and the only proof I need that there is something more powerful than I am looking out for my best interests. So many stars had to align in order for Hailey and me to cross paths. I pulled a hamstring just in time to end up on our team's physical therapist's schedule on the last day of Hailey's internship, mere minutes before she was to walk out the door and never come back.

Even securing the internship in the first place was a long shot for an eighteen-year-old. Hailey was the youngest applicant to ever score the position. Her college advisor tried to discourage her, insisting writing the internship essay would be a waste of her time, but Hailey applied anyway.

She's stubborn, my girl. And she believes in herself. And she isn't about to take no for an answer if she thinks there's even a shot in hell of convincing someone to say yes.

I'm not really surprised when my doorbell rings just after four o'clock and I open the door to find Hailey standing on my welcome mat, wearing her raincoat even though there isn't a cloud in sight.

No, I'm not surprised, but I am instantly awash in warring emotions. Will the ex-boyfriend is thrilled to see her, but Will the submissive professor isn't happy about having his direct order ignored. He's not happy at all, and at least for now, he's the one calling the shots with Hailey.

So instead of throwing open the door and ushering her inside the way I usually would, I cross my arms, lean against the doorframe, and cast a glance down my nose. "Is it Monday, Miss Marks?"

Trapping her bottom lip between her teeth, Hailey

shakes her head slowly back and forth. "No, Mr. Saunders, it's not Monday, but I have a compelling argument as to why we really should reschedule lesson two for today. I made a list and everything." She threads her fingers together in front of her and rocks back and forth in her high-heeled pumps, blinking her big blue eyes. "So I was hoping I could come in, and present my evidence?"

"You could have texted the list," I say, not budging an inch. "Or emailed."

"Well, yes, you're right... I could have..." The skin around her eyes tightens, and I can see her wheels spinning as she tries to figure out a way to avoid obeying orders. She's cute as hell, and a part of me wants nothing more than to pull her inside and show her how much I've missed her during the few hours we've been apart, but that would be rewarding poor behavior.

Instead I say, "Why don't you do that, and we'll discuss your list via the proper channels."

A stricken expression flashes across her features. "No, please, Will. I'm sorry I bent the rules, but I'm new. Which means I need more one-on-one instruction, not less. If you let me come in, maybe you can teach me some new strategies. Ways to helps me stay disciplined in times of temptation."

"The best way to resist temptation is not to let it in the door to begin with." I stand firm even though Exboyfriend Will is shouting for me to quit being a dick and let her in. "I'm going to have to ask you to leave, Curious."

Hurt flickers in her eyes, but it's soon banished by

determination and that stubborn jut of her chin I know so well. "But I don't want to leave. And I don't think you want me to leave, either."

"No, I don't want you to leave," I answer honestly, "but I do want you to learn to respect boundaries I've put in place for your protection."

"But I don't need to be protected from you." She fiddles with the belt holding her coat closed. "And I'm ready for another lesson. I promise. I even came prepared..." Slowly, she slips the tie loose and parts the front of her coat, revealing tiny white lace panties, a white lace bra, and nothing else.

Instantly, I'm hard, my cock thick and aching behind the fly of my jeans, but I'm not amused. Just a few days into her training, and she's already trying to top from the bottom, already trying to take the reins and see how far I'll let her steer us off course.

But this isn't my first time at the power-play games, and I'm not about to give away the upper hand so easily. That isn't what Hailey really wants, anyway, not deep down. She's simply testing my limits, my word, and making sure it's safe to put herself in my hands.

Which means, no matter how much I want to indulge her and my own need to have her under me again, there's only one way to handle this situation.

Lips pressed into a tight line, I reach out and calmly, but firmly, close her coat, wrap the tie back around her waist, and secure it with a knot. When I'm finished I step back and point to the end of the hall, "Go stand by the potted plant with your nose to the window."

Her eyes go wide. "What?"

"Go stand by the potted plant with your nose to the window until I give you permission to go home. Mr. Stubblefield and the Yangs are out of town, so no one should bother you, but if anyone asks what you're doing, tell them you're admiring the view and leave it at that. Everyone who works in the building knows you're on my approved guest list."

"You're kidding," Hailey says with a shaky laugh, but the worry flickering across her features makes it clear she knows I'm not.

I shake my head, which summons a sigh from her lips.

"Shit," she mutters. "I screwed up. I'm sorry."

"You did. It happens. Just take your punishment like a good girl, and we'll move forward from here."

Her nose wrinkles, and her upper lip curls into an irritated squiggle. "I don't like being a good girl. I'm a grown woman, not a girl."

"Noted," I say, fighting a smile. "We can see if you enjoy being a bad grown woman better than a good girl tomorrow during our scheduled lesson. But tonight, you need to take your punishment." And with that, I shut the door in her face, grinning at the affronted gasp from the other side.

I adore Hailey, and in real life, I definitely prefer not to get on her bad side.

But this isn't real life, this is the game, and Dominant Will enjoys teaching a submissive her place, especially a hard-to-handle submissive. Dominant Will can't wait to see if Hailey obeys orders, already plotting what kind of punishment she'll receive tomorrow night if she refuses to do as she's told.

The thought of Hailey draped over my lap with her ass bare to the flat of my hand is so erotic, in fact, that I almost hope she chooses to disobey.

But when I peek outside ten minutes later, she's there at the end of the hall, with her trench coat wrapped around her and her cute little nose pressed to the window, and I immediately realize I was wrong.

Seeing her taking her punishment like a good submissive is way better than any other outcome. Knowing that she's on board with this, on board with my control and my rules and me leading the way through this new-to-us experience, is a turn-on like nothing else. Because it means there's real hope. Hope that Hailey is enjoying this experiment as much as I am, hope that we'll be able to make power exchange something that's organic to our relationship, hope that before too long we'll be a couple again and that it will be the two of us against the world, the way it's meant to be.

I'm so fucking happy—elated really—that it's hard as hell to shut the door. I want to touch her, kiss her, to show her with my body how proud I am of her for being brave enough to put herself into my hands.

But that will have to wait until tomorrow night. If I'm going to maintain control of my headstrong girl, I have to show her that when it comes to the game, my word isn't to be questioned.

Instead of slipping outside to surprise her, I wait exactly forty-three minutes—a punishment weighty enough for her to know that I mean business, but short enough to keep her legs from going numb—and shoot off a text—*Thank you for your obedience, Curious. You can go home now, and I'll call you tomorrow to talk details for Lesson Two.*

After a beat, bubbles fill my screen, indicating her impending response. The bubbles go on and on, making me wonder what kind of opus she's writing, but when the text pops through, it's only four words: *Okay. See you tomorrow.*

I bite my lip, but I can't resist replying, *You're taking this awfully well.*

Hailey shoots back an angry cat emoji, making me laugh, followed by, *That clearly wasn't my ideal outcome, but...I get it. At least I think I get it.*

What do you think you get? I ask.

You're serious, she replies. *This may be a game, but it's a game with rules you take seriously, and you expect me to do the same. If I don't, this won't work. And it won't be as much fun, either.*

My lips curve. *If you were having fun out there, I wasn't doing my job properly.*

No, I wasn't having fun. I was pretty pissed at first. She sends through three angry cats in a row, followed by a ball of fire and a skull and crossbones emoji. *But while I was standing here with my nose pressed to the window, I realized that—in addition to feeling mortified and worried someone we know might show up in the hall and ask what the hell I was doing—I also felt...safe. It's nice knowing exactly what to expect. I follow the rules and things go smoothly; I disobey and there are consequences. It's like the rules are a safety net, even when I break them...if that makes any sense.*

I lean against the wall near the door, wishing I were outside having this conversation with her instead of locked on my side of the divide. But she's right, the rules are important, so I let my thumbs do the talking. *It makes complete sense and I couldn't agree more. The rules are our safety net. The more you see me obeying the rules, the more you know you can trust me. The more you trust me, the freer you'll feel to let go. And the more you let go, the more fun we can have together.*

Bubbles fill the screen for a good thirty seconds, but again, her eventual reply is only two sentences long. *I like the sound of that. See you tomorrow, sir.*

This time I have to move away from the door, striding deeper into the apartment to keep from reaching for the knob and joining her in the hall. I want to kiss her sweet, obedient mouth. I want to squeeze her ass and tell her how proud I am of her for being open to this change, this adventure, this new way of loving each other. I want to carry her to my bed and celebrate her success with half a dozen orgasms and an all-night cuddle session.

Instead, I remember the rules and tap out, *See you then, sweetheart. Get home safe,* and then I head out to the balcony, watching the street until I see her blond head emerge from the lobby door and head west toward the river.

"Tomorrow, Curious," I murmur, electricity prickling across my skin as I start whipping up a lesson plan she'll never forget.

CHAPTER 14

HAILEY

*D*espite being plagued by a level of sexual frustration I haven't experienced in ages—maybe *ever*—I'm shocked to find that, once again, I sleep like the dead, and awake filled with energy and ready to take on a grey and drizzly Monday.

After all, the faster I get through my work, phone calls, and a hefty number of emails, the sooner I'll be headed over to Will's for Lesson Two.

Or maybe he'll want to come back to your place, since your headboard is so tying-you-up friendly...

The thought makes me blush, grin, and hurry through breakfast so I can tidy up the apartment and put clean sheets on the bed, just in case. I'm still not completely comfortable with submissive Hailey's giddiness at the thought of being tied up, but I'm enjoying myself too much to care.

Even yesterday, standing with my nose pressed to

the window, taking my medicine for disobeying Will's orders, was strangely erotic.

The knowledge that I was standing there because Will had told me to, and that he was monitoring my obedience, thinking of me, controlling me even though he was nowhere in sight, was almost unbearably arousing. My nipples were hard throughout the duration of my punishment, and by the time I left his building, my panties were wet.

And we won't even discuss what happened when I got home and finally had my vibrator in hand and the privacy to take the edge off.

Suffice it to say those batteries don't have much life left in them.

Neither did I by the time I'd fantasized about Will taking me from behind in the hallway of his building, with my coat shoved up around my waist, the city of Portland spread out beneath us, and the chance that we might get caught making my blood rush in a way that had me questioning what I'm into sexually.

Do I want to get it on in a public place? Would the risk of being discovered really make me come so hard my knees would be reduced to jelly?

I have no idea, but my lessons with Will have put all sorts of new things on my radar, filling my head with terrifying, exhilarating, bliss-inducing possibilities.

At work, I expect to be distracted and on edge as I wait for word from Will, but I'm a productivity power-house. I'm so focused that by the time my first students arrive at nine-thirty, I've already answered all my work-related emails, shot off an order for new crash mats, and called the cleaning service to schedule the semi-annual gym deep clean.

I'm just Hailey at work—not submissive Hailey—but the sense of calm and safety that filled me yesterday lingers throughout my day. Shutting off the constantly vigilant side of myself to experiment with Will seems to have quieted my hyperawareness in general, and I marvel at how much easier it is to focus.

I've always assumed that restless, constant assessment made me an alert and productive human being, but by the time Will's phone call comes through after my three o'clock class, I'm rethinking things even more radical than my sexual preferences.

"I've had one of my best work days ever," I confess to Will, tucking into my office for privacy as the girls from my pre-teen class gather their things. "I've been so calm and focused, getting twice as much done in half the time. It's blowing my mind a little."

"In the good way, I hope," Will says, a smile in his voice. "It's like that for me, too. The game improves my overall focus. I always play hockey better the day after a scene."

My brow furrows. "Wow. So if we'd been doing this sooner, you might have won an Art Ross trophy by now?"

He laughs. "Nah. I haven't been playing at that level yet. But maybe this season. I'm already off to a good start, scoring big. Coach says I'm hitting my prime."

I perch on the edge of my desk with a grin. "Oh, I would agree. You're definitely in your prime."

"Stop," Will warns. "Or I'm going to have to come

over there and fuck you on your desk before we go out tonight."

Nerve endings humming at the thought, I whisper, "Well, I am sitting on my desk right now... But wouldn't that be against the rules, sir?"

"Not if the desk-banging was part of your punishment, Curious. Tonight's lesson is all about seeing if you enjoy being bad, remember?"

"I do remember. And I can't wait." I tap my toes on the carpet in a spontaneous dance of anticipation that isn't like me. But then, maybe I don't know myself as well as I think I do. If these lessons accomplish nothing else, they've certainly broadened my horizons. "So what time am I seeing you, sexy?"

"Five-thirty. I'll bring dinner over to your place." He clears his throat before adding, "I can't wait. I missed you last night."

"I missed you, too." I smile, chest warm and full, overflowing with hope, happiness, and anticipation.

"Good. Oh, and Hailey, I want you waiting by the door when I arrive, all right?"

I hum my agreement. "Of course, sir."

"On your knees," he adds, making my pulse spike, "wearing that little white sundress I like, with no panties on underneath. No bra, either."

My eyes close as arousal dumps into my bloodstream, making my skin feel too tight and my soft cotton workout clothes suddenly too rough. "All right. I can do that, sir."

"Perfect." He sighs, the hunger in the sound sending tingles prickling up my thighs. "It's been a long day. I'm looking forward to seeing my good girl waiting for me when I get home. I don't have the patience for disobedience tonight. If I came home to a disobedient submissive tonight, I would be very upset."

"Oh, no, we wouldn't want that," I murmur, lips curving in a wicked grin as I read his subtext. "I'll be good, sir, I promise."

He makes a sound I've never heard before—somewhere between a growl and a chuckle—and says, "Goodbye, Curious. See you soon."

"Soon," I promise, teeth digging into my bottom lip as I tap the button to end the call. Soon, soon, soon...

Soon I will be in Dominant Will's presence again.

Soon I will be in his arms and under his command.

Soon I will find out whether I prefer to be a good girl or a bad one...

CHAPTER 15

I've never been into head games—I prefer to lay my cards on the table in my business and personal relationships—but by the time I get home from work and grab a quick shower, I'm not myself anymore.

I'm submissive Hailey, the naughty bad girl who's dying for her master to show her who's boss.

After I've dried off from my shower and rubbed the honeysuckle lotion Will loves into every inch of my skin, I skip the bra and panties beneath my cotton sundress. But even though it's nearly five thirty, I don't pad across my apartment to kneel beside the door. Instead, I unlock the door and turn the knob, leaving it slightly ajar as I cross back to the kitchen table, where the mail I fetched on my way upstairs is spread out across the rough wooden surface.

Nerve endings humming, I stand beside the table,

ears straining and heart already pumping faster simply because I know Will is close.

Closer...

Soon to be closest...

When the elevator dings softly from down the hall at exactly five-thirty on the dot, my heart leaps into my throat, and my head begins to spin. I can't remember the last time I was this excited, this giddy with anticipation, this deliciously scared.

What, oh what, is my sir going to do to me when he realizes what a bad girl I've been?

Blood rushing and cheeks hot, I trap the insides of my cheeks between my teeth, biting back a smile as I lean over, pretending to be reading my electric bill as I arch my back enough to ensure my sundress rides up the backs of my thighs. As the door opens behind me, a light breeze gusts over the bottom of my bare ass cheeks, making my already slick pussy swell in response.

And then Will says, "You're not where I told you to be, Hailey," in a deep, dangerous voice, and my knees go weak.

I'm so instantly, wildly turned on that I have to brace my arms on the table to remain upright as I glance over my shoulder at Will. "I'm sorry, sir. I forgot," I say, my voice shaking and the temptation to smile a distant memory.

Will looks as angry as he sounded, and for a brief moment, I wonder if I've made a mistake.

But before I can remember what my safe word is, let alone use it, Will is across the room, shoving me down onto the table. My gasp of surprise becomes a moan of arousal as he pins me against the wood with his hips, letting me feel how hard he is behind the fly of his jeans. The rough denim against my sensitive skin is so erotic that the room is already spinning, even before Will lifts my skirt, shoving it up around my waist.

"Then I need to do something to help improve your memory," he says, one hand braced on the table beside my face as the other skims down my belly and between my legs, finding the center of the electrical storm currently overwhelming my nervous system.

"Please forgive me, sir," I whisper. "I'm sorry."

"Not yet, but you will be, sweetheart." Will grinds his hand gently, but firmly, against my clit as he rocks into me from behind, jeans grinding into my increasingly drenched flesh. "Now, usually I would ask you to tell me when you're about to come, so I would know when to stop fucking you with my hand. But I don't trust you to be a good girl right now, Hailey. So these are the rules for tonight." He intensifies the pressure of the heel of his hand on the top of my sex, making me gasp as he adds, "If you come before I give you permission, I'm going to spank you, sweetheart. I'm going to spank you hard until your ass is red and it will hurt to sit down tomorrow. Do you understand me?"

I whimper in response, already so close to coming it's clear I'm going to fail this test. I'm going to get a spanking—there's no doubt in my mind. The knowledge is terrifying and thrilling, making my pulse spike again as Will knees my thighs farther apart, granting him easier access to the slickness between my legs.

"Answer me, Hailey." He thrusts against me from behind, his hips pushing me forward, sending my clit rolling back and forth over his hand. "I need to know that you understand the consequences if you come before you've been told to come."

"Y-yes, sir," I stammer, as I fight the wave of pleasure swelling inside of me. "But please, stop. Stop touching me there or I—"

"Stop touching you where?" he asks, his breath hot in my hair as he leans closer. "Your pussy, Hailey? Is that where you want me to stop touching you?"

"Y-yes," I reply, though that's the last thing I want. I don't want him to stop; I want him to go and go and go. I want him to push his jeans down around his knees, free his cock, and shove into me from behind while his hand stays exactly where it is. I want to come with his thickness buried deep inside me, my body locking down on his hard, hot, oh-so-perfect...

So perfect...

Oh God, so fucking perfect, I can't—

I won't, but I can't stop I can't—

I come with an anguished cry, a sound of celebration and regret that's barely escaped my lips when Will's hand lands on my ass. The first few blows barely register —I'm too busy soaring, exploding, bursting into stardust and scattering throughout the reaches of the galaxy.

But by the time I start to come down from my release, I become very aware of what those steady, merciless blows are doing to my body.

"Oh God, Will," I gasp, my bottom on fire in a way

that isn't unpleasant at all. It hurts, but it also...hums. It's also hot, making my voice rougher as I groan, "Oh, God."

"Sir, Hailey." He slaps me harder, and I cry out. "Remember your manners during the game."

"Yes, sir. Oh, sir, I don't— I can't—" I moan low in my throat, words failing me as my head spins and a heavy sensation spreads through my core, arousal building so fast I feel like a balloon about to burst.

And it's all because of this pain, this pleasure, this wicked sweet bliss lifting me higher and higher, until I'm arching into Will's hand, welcoming each blow with a cry as my pussy swells. Soon I'm bruised with longing and so desperate for his cock tears are stinging the backs of my eyes.

"Don't come, Hailey." The hand between my legs shifts, making me gasp as his fingers glide inside me. I shudder, my inner walls pulling tight around the welcome invasion as he warns, "Wait until I give you permission, baby, or I'm going to have to punish you again. And I'd hate to do that, to have to spank you somewhere even more soft and vulnerable than this sweet ass."

I brace my hands beneath my shoulders, fingers clawing into the table as I fight the desire swelling inside me, the dark wave that threatens to sweep me under the moment I let down my guard.

"Please, sir," I beg, sweat breaking out along the valley of my spine as Will's fingers drive deeper, demanding my surrender with every thrust into my drenched pussy. "Please help me, please. Oh, God, sir, I'm going to come if you don't stop, I'm going to—"

This time I come so hard I slip past the boundaries of my own skin. The ecstasy rocketing through my veins transports me to some higher plane, where I ride a nirvana wave for what feels like forever before I finally ease back into my body. I blink fast, shocked to find myself lying on the floor beside the table with Will kneeling between my legs and no memory of how I got there.

My lips part, but before I can say a word, Will strips off his shirt and reaches for the close of his jeans, and all I can do is groan in approval.

God, he's perfect, every hard inch of him from his drool-worthy chest and powerful shoulders to his chiseled abs and those oh-so-lickable indentions on either side of his hips. And of course, those nine pulsing inches that are my favorite inches of all.

I spread my legs and reach for him, wordlessly begging for him to come to me, to lengthen himself over me and push inside me, putting an end to the terrible emptiness dragging between my thighs.

But he simply shakes his head and reaches down, gripping the base of his cock, "Not yet, baby. Punishment first, pleasure when you learn to do as you're told. Now, spread your legs wider for me. Show me every inch of you."

I hesitate a moment, still too dazed from my second orgasm to understand why he's denying me the connection I crave, and Will insists, "Now, Hailey," and slaps my ass with his free hand, making me yip in surprise.

That swat hurt more than the ones before, making me think it really might hurt to sit down tomorrow. But I can't worry about that now. I don't have the headspace for worry. I only have room for Will and doing whatever it takes to convince him to put me out of my misery.

I spread my legs wider, breath coming faster as I bare my embarrassingly wet sex to Will's gaze. But he clearly isn't repulsed by how much I want him. As his gaze falls between my thighs, he clenches his jaw and growls low in his throat, that animal sound of need making me feel sexier than I have in my entire life.

"Fuck, yes, Hailey," he says, gripping the base of his cock tighter. "I love seeing you swollen and dying for me to fuck you. Are you dying for me to fuck you yet, baby?"

"Yes, sir." My thighs begin to tremble from the strain of keeping them spread so wide. "Oh, please, sir."

"Not yet, sweetheart," he says. "But soon. Hands behind your knees and pull them up, I want you wide open to me for your punishment."

I do as he asks without thinking, so desperate to win his approval that the 'punishment' part escapes my attention until Will lifts his cock and brings it down sharply between my legs, hitting my clit hard enough to send pleasure-pain zinging straight into my core.

I cry out, and he hits me again, making my hips jerk involuntarily in response. "Hold still, baby, or I'll use my hand instead, and I don't think you're ready for that."

I whimper, but I force myself to lie still as he strikes me again and then again, thumping each side of my pussy before returning to my clit. This time, however, it doesn't hurt when he strikes that sensitized place, it sizzles. I gasp as he repeats the pattern—left, right, center, left, right, center, until my chest is heaving, my nipples rock-hard beneath the thin fabric of my dress, and I'm so close to coming again that tears leak from the corners of my eyes.

"Beautiful. You're so fucking beautiful," Will pants. "Dress off, Hailey. Take it off, baby. I need your nipples in my mouth."

Struggling a bit to free the fabric trapped beneath my shoulders, I rip my dress over my head with trembling arms. The feel of the cotton brushing over my nipples is enough to make me cry out in surprise. My skin is so hypersensitive that for a moment I'm worried it might hurt for Will to touch me there. But I should have known better.

When he bends forward, taking my nipple into his mouth and sucking oh-so-gently on the taut flesh, I cry out my soul-deep appreciation for this man who knows me so well, who can read me so perfectly, and who realizes exactly how much I can take before I fall to pieces.

"Oh, please, oh, please," I chant as Will licks and sucks, alternating between my nipples until they're both slick and aching and my entire body feels like a wound in need of relief. Of release. "Oh please…"

"Please, what, angel?" Will's mouth covers mine, making me groan as he kisses me so hard and deep I lose all sense of up or down. "Please what," he groans against my lips, "tell me what you want."

"I want you. Now, inside me, now," I force out in a voice I barely recognize.

But I barely remember who I am.

I'm not *I* anymore, I'm *His*.

Or at least I want to be. God, I want to be.

"I'm dying for you to fuck me," I pant, driving my fingers into his hair and fisting them as he kisses me again and the fever-hot head of his cock butts lightly against where I need him so desperately. "Oh yes. Please, Will, please, I'm dying. I'm—"

He shoves into me with a sharp thrust that banishes all the words from my mouth and the thoughts from my head. Instantly, I'm filled with a mixture of relief and pleasure so intense it's all I can do to hold on tight to his shoulders and lift my hips frantically to meet his as he drives hard and fast inside me.

There is none of our usual build up, no easing into each other. He claims me with that first merciless stroke and continues as he began. He fucks me so hard my ass slides across the hardwood floor, so hard that there is pain mixed with my pleasure, but it's the best pain, the sweetest pain, so incredible and intense that when Will groans into my ear, "Come now, Hailey. Come on your cock, baby," I'm gone in a flash, a heartbeat.

I come again, crying out into Will's mouth as my body locks down on his cock.

He groans in response and fucks me impossibly harder, chanting, "Yes, baby, yes, baby, yes," against my lips as I come and come, my pleasure unfolding like the most intricate origami ever creased into being.

And then, just as I'm reaching the peak, Will shoves

his hips forward one last time, calling out my name as he comes, buried so deep inside of me that I can I feel him everywhere, all at once. I wrap my arms and legs around him, holding on tight as his balls pulse against my ass and echoes of his orgasm soak through my skin making me soar all over again.

Our sweat-slick bodies writhe against each other until the bliss fades to a sweet buzz and then a happy hum and finally we lie still on the floor, too spent to do anything but sigh softly against each other's throats as our pulses slow. Gradually, enough awareness returns that I realize that the floor is hard and my tailbone is bruised, and I shift slightly beneath him.

"Yes, ma'am," he murmurs in response to my unspoken request, holding me close as he rolls over, moving me on top without disrupting our connection.

I sigh, happy to have him still inside me, even if he's softer now and there's so much wet heat between us I know he'll slip free soon.

"Good?" he asks, brushing my hair over my shoulder.

"Bad," I reply, my voice thick and lazy. "I like being bad, sir."

Will chuckles. "I thought you might."

"What about you?" I lift my head, propping my chin on my fist as I gaze down at him. "Did you like punishing me?"

His eyes darken, the hunger and appreciation in them making me shiver. "Like it? What do you think?"

Shy, but certain, I whisper, "I think you loved it."

"I did love it." His palms skim up my thighs to cup

my bare ass, gently squeezing my tender flesh, making my nipples tighten in response. "I loved feeling you get so wet... Knowing it was because you were loving every minute as much as I was..."

I pull in a breath, my pulse speeding faster as desire floods through me like a drug. I swallow, throat working as I work up the courage to confess, "I already want to do it again, Will. I want you to punish me again."

"Well, you have been a bad girl," he says, grip tightening on my ass. "You were supposed to meet me kneeling. I had plans for kneeling Hailey, and you ruined them. I'm not sure one spanking is enough to make up for how disappointing that was."

I bite my lip, clit pulsing as his cock begins to thicken inside of me. "I think you're right, sir. I have a belt you can use if you'd like."

Will's eyes dance into mine. "Oh, I would like, Curious. I would like that very much."

Turns out, I'm also a fan of the belt. A big fan.

Such a fan that by the time I wake up cozy in the circle of Will's arms on Tuesday morning, my backside is so tender it hurts to sit down.

But I like that, too. I like that I can't slide into my chair at work without a visceral reminder of what Will and I did the night before, without remembering who I belong to. We're not officially back together, but I feel closer to Will than ever.

So close that by the time we finish our next few lessons, all it takes is a single heated look from my man in Dom mode to make me wet.

To make me melt, to make me wild and shameless and so eager for more that we fly through Will's planned curriculum in just two weeks and begin to experiment.

He takes me from behind on the balcony as the stars come out, unbuttoning my shirt to the waist so anyone looking hard enough could see my breasts bobbing softly as he makes me come. We try out handcuffs and bound ankles and a toy that sends soft electric shocks through my nipples that drives me absolutely out of my mind with hunger.

We venture into forbidden territory, and I learn that butt stuff isn't a hard limit for me, after all.

I actually enjoy butt stuff, and the moment Will takes me there for the first time—his gaze locked on mine in the reflection in the bathroom mirror as he bends me over the sink and pushes into my well-lubed backside—is so hot I know I'll never forget it.

I will never forget any of these lessons in what it feels like to be both vulnerable and powerful, dominated and liberated, powerless and so completely free that for the first time in my life I'm not worried about being in control.

I give up my control without a fight, crossing out all the items on my "no-fly" list and laying it at Will's feet.

Goodbye rules.

Hello, Sir.

CHAPTER 16

**From the texts of Hailey Marks
and Sabrina Marks**

Three weeks later

Hailey: Good morning, Little Sis.
I have a question for you.
I've been wondering—Does it ever weird you out?
When you take a step back and look at all the big
changes you've made in your life in such a short amount
of time?

Sabrina: Wha? Srsly? Wha tm is it...

Hailey: It's almost eight. So yeah, like...when you wake
up on a chilly October morning like this one and realize

how different your life is now than it was a year ago?
When you were modeling in Milan and rolling around
on the beaches of Antigua? Do you feel like a stranger
has shoplifted your life?
Or does it feel right?
Or strange and right at the same time?

Sabrina: Didn't anyone ever tell you there's a rule
against Deep Thoughts before ten a.m.? Especially on
Mondays? And especially when the person you're
asking probing questions only got off work six
hours ago?
The bar is open until two a.m. on Sundays.

Hailey: Oh man, I'm sorry.
I didn't mean to wake you.
Why didn't you turn your ringer off before you went
to sleep?

Sabrina: Are you trying to make me feel like a loser? Or
is that just a groovy side effect of whatever crawled up
your skirt this morning?

Hailey: I'm not wearing a skirt, I'm wearing leggings
and a tank top so I can teach young women to kick ass.
And of course I'm not trying to make you feel like a
loser! I'm so proud of you for living your life on your
terms and honoring your truth even when most people
your age would have stuck with modeling no matter
how miserable it made them, just for the travel bennies
and free clothes.

Sabrina: You're sounding old again. Like mom. You might as well just go get pregnant right now and have some babies. You're destined to be a fussy mom type who refuses to let your kids eat junk food and nags them about the dangers of sleeping too close to their cell phones.

Hailey: Electromagnetic radiation isn't something I made up, you know. It's real. And it's bad for you. And you shouldn't sleep with your phone.

Sabrina: I love you. You're a cute old lady.

Hailey: I love you, too. And you're a brat. Go back to sleep, I'll talk to you later.

Sabrina: No, I'm up now. Pondering your question has banished sleep. So…yes, it is weird sometimes. I look around and see how much things have changed and have a hard time believing this is my life. But it's also right. I'm so much happier. So, weird and right is my answer.

Hailey: So you think the two can coexist?

Sabrina: Absolutely. But now I'm curious to know what inspired your line of questioning? Are things with Will finally getting weird?

Hailey: No comment.

Sabrina: Ewwww!! They are getting weird, aren't they! I mean, you're three weeks into your lessons now, right? It's about time things started getting super-duper kinky winky. So what tripped your freak-out reflex?

Hailey: I said no comment.

Sabrina: Did he tie you up? Try to pee on you in a sexual way? Make you dress up in a naughty school girl outfit and pretend he was going to get you pregnant before graduation?

Hailey: I'm not going to touch any of that except to say your reading habits worry me sometimes and that pee is for the toilet.

Sabrina: Well *I* know that. But I'm not a Big Bad Dirty Dom.
I have to confess it's hard to imagine Will being mean to someone, even in a pretend way. He's such a sweetheart.

Hailey: He's not mean. He's…wonderful. So incredibly wonderful.

Sabrina: Aw, you're falling in love with Will again!

Hailey: I never fell *out* of love with him, Bree.
Love was never the problem.
Other stuff was the problem.
But now I'm pretty sure I'm into the other stuff, too, but

it's still so new that sometimes I get freaked out and wonder what the heck I'm doing. I mean, yes, I'm having a blast and the best sex of my life, but...

Well, there's a part of me that still feels like I'm trying on a pricey pair of sky-high heels or something. I like the look of them, but I'm not sure if I want to plunk down three hundred bucks and take them home, where I'll be obligated to wear them at least twice a week to justify paying that much for them.

I don't know if power exchange is something I'm ready to commit to forever, you know?

Sabrina: Then don't do it forever. Have fun with it as long as it's fun, and when it stops being fun, tell Will you want to take a break.

Hailey: But that's not fair to him. I can't promise to make this part of our relationship going forward and then back out. I need to know for sure if I'm ready to sign on the submissive dotted line.

But it's just still so new and...I feel new, too.

Sabrina: How so?

Hailey: I don't know. It's like questioning one part of my life opened the door for all these other questions. I'm second-guessing things I've taken for granted for years and wondering who I really am. If my opinions can change so drastically on so many things, am I even the same person I was before? Or someone completely different?

Sabrina: Wow. That makes my head hurt.

Hailey: Tell me about it. I think I'm having a quarter-life crisis.

Sabrina: Lol. You are not. You're just going through a growing spurt. It's good for you. We're supposed to keep growing, you know. You don't reach adulthood and suddenly have everything all figured out forever.

Hailey: I know.
I just never expected this to hit me so hard.
Everything feels different except the way I feel about Will. And that feels like…coming home.
Like coming home after months lost at sea. He's that first glimpse of land.

Sabrina: The first bite of chocolate cake after dieting for three months so your abs will show on the cover of the swimsuit issue.

Hailey: I can't imagine going without cake for that long, but yes, I bet it's just like that. So good it almost makes me want to cry. I'm just so happy and relieved and grateful to have him in my life again.

Sabrina: Aw, you're going to make me cry! That's so sweet!

Hailey: Seriously, I don't know how much longer I can

wait to tell him that I want to be with him again. I want to be Us again. Surely, even if the weird feeling sticks around for a while—even forever—it will be worth it to know I'm never going to have to live without him again. Right?

Sabrina: Okay, now hold up a second. It would be worth pretending for the rest of your life to be something you're not? Really?

Hailey: I don't know! I just miss him so much, Bree. I miss being happy without having to try so hard. When Will and I were broken up, it felt like I spent half my life fighting off the blues, boosting myself up with exercise or meditation or forced fun outings to go see sketch comedy or take in the new exhibit at the museum. Not being miserable had become so much fucking work.
But when I'm with Will, I just...float.

Sabrina: So float, woman. Enjoy yourself and give the new stuff some time. You two will figure it out. There's no need to rush. Just go with the flow and try not to overthink everything the way you always do. Some things can't be sorted out with your head, Hailey Rae. Some things have to be understood with your heart. And yet still others must be soaked up via your vagina.

Hailey: That's sweet, smart, and gross all at the same time.

Sabrina: You're welcome. I'm going back to sleep now. I'm going to try to make your two-thirty class, but if I'm not there, don't worry. I'm considering staying in my pajamas all day, playing records, and catching up on my smut reading. I've been buried in Man's Search for Meaning for a week, and I could use a break from wanting to cry because I'm so simultaneously inspired and filled with empathy.

Hailey: You're going to be a good therapist.

Sabrina: If I can keep from crying all the time. Speaking of crying, Creedence called me again last night.

Hailey: Wow. And he was crying?

Sabrina: No, I just wanted to talk about my love life for a change, and that seemed like an easy transition. He wasn't crying, but he *was* bummed that I'm sticking to my "just friends" policy. He wants another real date, and I'm inclined to give him one.

Hailey: What about the STD factor? I mean, that's a deal breaker, isn't it?

Sabrina: The STD has not been confirmed. It's hearsay at this point. And he's just so sexy, Hailey. Demanding and intense and poetically obsessed with me in the cute way, not the creepy way. I mean, we ended up talking on the phone for nearly an hour last night, and

I'm pretty sure I haven't done that since junior
high. So...

Hailey: So you're going to see him again.

Sabrina: I am. I know Will said he was bad news, but he
may have gotten flawed information. Our mutual friend
Shane is a great guy, but he's got a little thing for me,
I think.

Hailey: Shane Wallace?! Oh, he's so cute, Bree! And such
a sweetheart.
You should totally go out with him! You would have so
much fun together!
He's got a great sense of humor.

Sabrina: Yeah, I know, Hailey, I've been friends with
him for a long time. But he's a total jock, and I'm not a
jock girl. I'm into artistic, intellectual guys. Guys who
write music or poetry or read Rilke in German.

Hailey: Pale posers who wear a lot of black, have dark
circles under their eyes, and look skinnier in skinny
jeans than I do?

Sabrina: *dreamy sigh* Yes. Like vampires, but with
dirty hair.

Hailey: Well...whatever floats your boat, I guess.

Sabrina: Thatta girl. Go with the flow, be open to alternative ways of looking at the world, and you'll get through this new adventure with Will just fine.

Hailey: Just don't come crying to me when your bed is full of hipster crabs.

Sabrina: Lies. Those are dirty lies.

Hailey: And make sure he wraps it up. Twice. Just in case he's collected anything grosser than pubic parasites in his sexual travels.

Sabrina: La la la…not listening, there is no hateration in this dancery, sister.

Hailey: Fine, crazy. Just be safe. And get your butt to class today so I can give you a hug. I miss your face.

Sabrina: Will do. All the hugs.

Hailey: All the hugs.

CHAPTER 17

HAILEY

*A*fter the intensity of the weekend with Will—and of the past three weeks in general—this particular Monday seems to crawl like a snail crossing a salt plain against a seventy-degree headwind.

I'm still a lean, mean, focused machine, but I struggle to take proper form as seriously as usual and keep letting my students' little mistakes slide instead of forcing them to go back to the beginning of an exercise and take it at half speed until they get the sequence just right.

I've been teaching self-defense for years—all levels, from beginning to advanced—and no matter how many times I have to repeat the rules for engagement, I've never been bored a day at my job. Empowering women by teaching them how to protect themselves and the people they love is my passion, and passion doesn't get old.

Or so I'd thought...

But today I'm so laid back that my beginner girls end up climbing the ropes at the back of the gym and cackling like hyenas, and my teacher trainee class makes a motion to adjourn for coffee forty-five minutes into our sparring because they insist we could all use a double espresso before our afternoon sessions.

And though I *am* tired—I didn't get to sleep until after midnight last night—that's not why I'm half checked out. Will is the reason I'm suddenly wondering if I want to continue to teach full time or go back to school to get my master's in physical therapy.

Will and these damned, chaos-inducing submissive lessons...

If I weren't having so much fun, I would hate what they've done to my life.

But how can you hate something that results in multiple orgasms every single night?

"It's just not possible." I tug the ponytail holder from my hair and dig my fingers into my tight scalp. "But if you bring your B game tomorrow, you're not going to make a very good first impression on the pre-teens of Portland."

It's true. And I know better than to think the pre-teens will have mercy on me. Pre-teens have no mercy, which means it's time to woman up and make an adult decision, no matter how much I'm looking forward to seeing Will tonight.

As soon as I lock up the gym for the day, I tug my cell from my purse with a heavy heart and shoot him a text—*I'm sorry, but I'm going to have to beg off for tonight. My energy levels are low, and I need to be on top of my game tomorrow for my first school visits. Which means going home and going to bed early—and alone—tonight. Forgive me?*

After only a few moments, Will responds—*Of course. No forgiveness required, baby. I get it. Though, I will miss you.*

Sighing, I lean back against the sun-warmed bricks of the building as I type. *Me, too. I've been thinking about you all day.*

Good. Then I did my job last night.

I grin. *Yes, you did, sir. But just FYI, I'm totally ready to try the paddle next time I'm naughty. I'm dying to know what it feels like.* I bite my lip, debating the wisdom of saying more, but find myself unable to stop my thumbs from confessing, *I've been daydreaming about that all day, too. About what it will be like the first time. About whether I'll be bent over with my hands on the table or if you'll pull me across your lap or if I'll be tied to the headboard when the spanking starts...*

He sends over a sweating, panicked-looking emoji that makes me laugh. *Jesus, woman. You and your imagination are going to make me gray before my time. Or give me a hard-on that's not even a little bit locker room friendly.*

Oops, sorry, I write back. *Forgot you were at practice.*

Sure you did. This time he sends a devil emoji, making me feel oddly proud of myself. *Go home and get some sleep, Curious. We'll get back on track with our lesson plan on Thursday. I've got a late practice tonight and a publicity event tomorrow and then an away game on Wednesday.*

Disappointment flashes through my chest, and my lips turn down hard at the edges. *Sadness consumes me.*

Thursday is forever away. We'll be almost in week four by then.

Sadness consumes me, too, he replies, *but we still have two whole weeks left. And because I'm such an accommodating teacher, I'm willing to extend our sessions to a nine-week course, if needed, so we can complete the entire expanded curriculum at our leisure. I don't want to rush. I like taking my time with you.*

My heart melts, and my lips reverse their downward trajectory. "I like that, too," I murmur aloud. "I love it. And I love you. So much."

I want to say all of those things to Will—all of them and more—but instead I type out, *Ditto, baby. Thanks for being the best Discreet Gentleman ever.*

We're both still on uncertain ground. I know he loves me, too, and that we both want this to work for the long haul, but the fact remains that it might not. We might hit a brick wall during one of our final lessons and end up saying goodbye for good. And that will be less painful for both of us if we can keep the focus on our teacher/student relationship instead of our more complicated exes-who-don't-want-to-be-exes-anymore relationship.

It's my pleasure. Truly, Will responds after a moment. *I'll touch base with you Thursday morning, gorgeous. Be good while I'm gone. Or...*

Or what? I tap out, not ready to say goodbye. Thursday feels like it's eons away, and I can't help wishing that things were back the way they used to be between Will and me.

If they were, during our time apart I could look

forward to texts, video chats, and epic phone calls that last until well after midnight. Will and I always joked that we had some of our best conversations when there were hundreds of miles between us.

I'm staring at my phone, waiting for Will's next text when it starts to ring and Will's picture—a shot of him on the beach from our first vacation together years ago —appears on the screen.

I answer with a smile. "Or what? Don't keep me in suspense."

"Or you could come with me," he says, his voice pure temptation. "You could get Jill to cover your Wednesday afternoon class, and we can catch an early flight back from Vancouver on Thursday. Or you could get Jill to cover everything for the rest of the week, and we could stay in Vancouver for a few days, go shopping at Granville Island, wander around Stanley Park, make another trip across that suspension bridge that scares the hell out of you."

"You like scaring the hell out of me?" I ask, my blood fizzy in my veins.

"No, I like how tight you held onto me the first time we crossed that bridge. I want a repeat."

"I like holding on tight to you," I murmur, longing rising inside me. "But I shouldn't miss work. The new session just started a month ago."

"Yes, but most of the students aren't new, and you've been busting your ass non-stop for eleven months without a break. That's probably why you were tired today. You need a mental health day, some R and R."

I hum doubtfully even as my smile widens. "I don't

think so. I'm pretty sure the reason I was tired was that a very demanding man kept me kneeling on the bathroom floor until almost one in the morning."

"You looked so pretty there, I couldn't help myself. I've been thinking about that all day, baby, the way you looked in those tiny red panties and nothing else, with your nipples swollen from my kisses."

The arousal inspired by his words is so intense and immediate that I have no choice but to lean more of my weight against the wall. I couldn't stand up straight right now if I tried. "Don't," I whisper. "Or you're going to have me on my knees again outside the gym. You know the dirty talk makes me crazy."

"That wasn't dirty talk, baby," he says. "Dirty talk would be ordering you to make your pussy wet for me right now. So why don't you do that for me? Go back into the gym, lock the door, go into your office, and take off your clothes. Play with your nipples until I call you back, and then I'll tell you what I want you to do next."

My lips part on a reply, but before I can speak, a soft beep-beep sounds in my ear, indicating that he's ended the call.

I huff in frustration, my cheeks hot and my pussy even hotter. A part of me is dying to do exactly what Will ordered me to do in that Deep Dom voice of his, but I wasn't joking about needing the night off. I need to get home, make a healthy dinner, and get some rest so I'll be in top form tomorrow. I don't need to spend another half hour or more at the gym or get sucked into playing a game I didn't agree to play.

This is the perfect chance for me to put this new aspect of our relationship to the test, to use that safe word I've been keeping in my back pocket for the day when things eventually get too intense for my personal comfort.

But this isn't too intense; it's simply an overreach.

Do I still use the safe word for that?

Frowning, I start to text Will, but before I can finish, a text from him pops through—*Hey, babe. I'm sorry. I got carried away. As soon as I hung up, I realized I shouldn't have taken things that far. You texted to say you needed rest, and it's my job to respect your boundaries. Not only to respect them, but to enforce them for you in the event a scene leaves you too wiped out to manage by yourself. I slipped. Forgive me?*

Anxiety fading instantly, I smile. *Of course I forgive you. No one's perfect.*

But I'm pretty close right? he shoots back.

I laugh, rolling my eyes as I type, *Don't push your luck, bossy pants. I'm headed for home and will let you know about the trip tomorrow morning. I need to mull it over and see if I think Jill can handle things on her own.*

After a moment he texts back, *Sounds good. Hope you decide to come. I'd love to have you all to myself for a few days. And seriously, thanks for your understanding and your trust and...everything else. The past three weeks have been so special to me, Hailey. You're so special to me.*

It's the closest either of us has gotten to confessing "I love you" out loud, and even though the words are typed, not spoken, they make me melt the same way they would have if Will had whispered them in my ear.

He's so special to me, too, and who knows when we'll get another chance to get away for a weekend? The season is just gearing up, and games and practices are going to start coming even closer together. If I don't run away with him now, we might have to wait until next summer, and who knows what will be going on with our lives then.

It's time to seize the day, to trust my impulsive side. Impulsive Hailey is the one responsible for getting Will back in my life and in my bed, and that's working out just fine so far. Might as well give her a chance to call the shots when it comes to work, as well.

Trusting my gut, I tap Will's number as I start around the building toward the street. He picks up on the first ring, his harsh whisper sexy in my ear, "I've gotta be back on the ice in two minutes, so if I have to hang up again don't be mad."

"This won't take long," I promise, hurrying on. "I just wanted to tell you that I'm a definite yes for the trip. If Jill can't cover the classes, I'll find someone else who can."

"Perfect," he says, clearly thrilled. "I'll book your flight."

"And I think I might want to go back to school," I blurt out, the words bursting from my lips before I realize I intend to speak them aloud. "To get my master's degree in physical therapy and work with athletes like I originally planned. Or maybe do something completely different and only work at the gym part-time. Is that crazy?"

"Not even a little crazy," he says. "It's sexy and awesome."

I laugh. "Second guessing my life choices is sexy and awesome?"

"Evolving is sexy and awesome. And I have no doubt you'll kick ass at whatever you decide to do next. You're a force of nature, Marks."

"You, too." My heart fills with gratitude and love and half a dozen other squishy emotions I don't have the time—or freedom—to adequately express right now, so I simply add, "Thank you for being you."

"Ditto," he says. "Text you later with flight details. Gotta go."

This time, the beep-beep of the line going dead doesn't make me feel frustrated or disconnected from Will. We're clearly on the same page in every way, from the big stuff to the little stuff, to everything in between. It makes me feel close to him, like he's walking beside me even though we're miles apart.

And that feels so good. That fish out of water feeling I texted Sabrina about this morning is still there—hovering at the back of my every thought, making the familiar streets of Portland look sharp and strange as I amble home through the early evening drizzle—but I'm starting to think that's not necessarily a bad thing.

I'm not losing myself; I'm evolving, like Will said. And evolving *is* sexy and awesome.

So sexy and awesome that I don't hesitate to swing into Cupid's Closet on my way home to buy something special for the trip. Predictable Hailey always let Will pick out her lingerie—he was good at it, and Predictable

Hailey figured it was logical to let him choose the fancy stuff since he was the one who would be helping her out of all those hooks and ribbons. Predictable Hailey didn't have much of an opinion on lingerie except that she enjoyed the way it made Will respond when she put it on.

But Impulsive Hailey liked the way that tiny red thong last night made *her* feel. She enjoyed dressing for the part of the naughty submissive who would spend most of her evening kneeling on the floor. She also enjoys the innocent potentialities of white lace and the secret thrill that comes from deciding whether or not to put on panties beneath her silky sleep shirt.

As I move about the store, thoughtfully considering my lingerie choices and how they might fit into a sexy weekend away with the man I love, I realize that Impulsive Hailey isn't the right name for this new me. She's not impulsive, she's simply curious, open-minded, awake to all the marvelous possibilities I'd been asleep to before.

I'd always thought that surviving cancer had made me stronger than other people—more driven and determined and unwilling to compromise when it came to my goals. And it has done all those things, but maybe, just maybe, it also made me a little rigid in the process. I was so determined not to waste a moment of my reclaimed life that I never gave myself the chance to slow down and question my course or tweak my game plan. I never gave myself the chance to become someone other than Hailey the Fighter, Hailey the Survivor.

Now, with Will, through these lessons, I'm realizing that I'm not just one person anymore. I'm so many different people, sometimes in the same day, in the same hour, and all of them have something to teach me about how to live the fearless, sexy, loving, fun, and fabulous life I want to live.

"Would you like to sign up for our mailing list so you'll get an email when we release our holiday collection?" the sales clerk asks as I sign the credit card slip for my new purchase, a lacy sheer bra and panty set I'm sure my man will love with every fiber of his dear, sweet, dirty and Dominant soul.

I smile, nodding my head. "Yes, please." A naughty holiday sounds perfect, and hopefully, by December twenty-fifth, Will and I will once again be sharing a home, a bed, and a Christmas tree.

CHAPTER 18

WILL

There are two types of killer whale pods—a residential pod, that feeds on fish and is a more social, less aggressive unit, and a transient pod, which resembles a pack of rabid wolves determined to rip apart any prey in their path.

Tonight, the Vancouver Canucks are the second type.

By the end of the first period, the cute little orca symbol on their jersey is starting to look a hell of a lot more menacing than it did before. By the end of the second period—when we're down by two and feeling the burn from playing a speed game marked by relentless forechecking—morale is in the shitter.

We head down the tunnel for the second intermission out of breath and cussing the great nation of Canada for nurturing the dark hearts of these fucking Canucks and their hotshot new head coach.

"I want to go home," Cruise whines, collapsing onto

the bench in the locker room with a wince. "My ass hurts. You know that muscle in your ass, but like on the side of your ass? That one. That one hurts. A lot."

"Shut up, Cruise," Petrov grumbles, clearly not in the mood for jokes after being beaten within an inch of his life by the Canuck offense. "No one wants to hear your bitching."

"Aw, you feeling the pain, Petrov?" Cruise pulls a sad face. "Well, maybe if you wouldn't hold onto the puck like it's your emotional support animal, you wouldn't be so cranky."

"Maybe if you'd get open," Petrov shoots back, "I wouldn't have to."

I look to Brendan to see if he's going to shut this down before good-natured ribbing becomes a pointless argument. But the captain's on the phone in the corner, probably talking to his wife, our PR manager Laura, who's eight months pregnant and no longer able to travel with him to away games. Considering Cruise is usually our other peacemaker, I take it upon myself to step in and redirect.

"You're both right," I say, leaning back against the wall near the water cooler. "The forwards need to offer more support, and the defense needs to unload the puck faster. With their aggressive system, there isn't time for overanalyzing every play. We need to keep it simple, streamlined, and stay as responsive as possible. We have to be completely focused and stay in the moment, or opportunities are going to keep passing us by."

"I feel like I'm in yoga class," Wallace says in a hushed voice, bringing a smile to Petrov's stormy face.

"Except your balls aren't hanging out," Cruise quips, sending a ripple of laughter through the room.

"I took care of that." Wallace frowns. "I wear spandex underneath my shorts now, so you guys won't get jealous."

"Thank God," Petrov says before gesturing to me. "Saunders is right, though. We can't move fast if we're playing on our heels or waiting for a perfect pass. We need to adapt to their game."

"They certainly aren't going to adapt to ours," Cruise agrees.

We discuss strategy for the next few minutes and head back onto the ice in a more optimistic frame of mind. Almost immediately, there's a noticeable difference in the quality of play, and first Cruise and then Nowicki light the lamp, sending us into overtime. Unfortunately, the home team nets the game winner after Wallace misses a poke check on a breakaway and an especially rabid killer whale pounces on the puck for a tap-in into the wide-open net.

It's a loss, but it's still a point toward the playoffs, and more importantly, it confirmed for me all over again that I'm playing with some of the best people in the league. I feel lucky to have spent my career thus far with such an excellent group of idiots, and admit I'm feeling a little sappy and emotional as I meet up with Hailey outside the exit to the Rogers Arena.

Her face lights up when she sees me even as her lips turn down. "You guys fought hard. You should be proud of that turnaround. It was inspiring to watch."

I smile, hopefully making it clear I don't intend to

pout about our loss. "*You're* inspiring to watch. Want to go order pizza and make out while we wait for our order?"

"Sounds perfect." Eyes bright, Hailey moves into my arms, tipping her head back to welcome my kiss.

I claim her mouth soft and slow, relishing each brush of her warm skin against mine, wondering if I'll ever get to the point where I take her kiss for granted again.

I hope I never do.

I hope I'm always this present, this focused on my girl, this committed to treasuring every single second with her.

"Hey, Will?" Hailey whispers, kissing me with the words because our mouths are still that close.

Perfectly close.

"Yes, my love," I say without thinking, forgetting for a second that I'm not allowed to say that to her anymore —not now, not yet.

I pull back, prepared to apologize and dismiss the slip with a grin and a shrug, but when I meet Hailey's soft gaze I dare to hope the time for keeping our distance is over. Instead of walking back, I push forward, my heart in my throat and everything I feel for her thickening my words, "Yeah, I said it. And I meant it. I love you, Hailey Marks. I love the woman you were and the woman you are and the incredible, curious, sexy, fearless person you're becoming. I don't want to miss a minute of you. Of us. And I don't want this to end in a few weeks."

"Me either," she says, her eyes shining. "So, you

think you might be open to being my sexy boyfriend again? If I promise to be very good and occasionally very bad?"

I nod slowly, chest filling with a storm of happiness as I pull her closer. "Yes. I want to be your sexy boyfriend. And I want you good, bad, and everything in between."

"But maybe bad tonight?" She arches her back until I'm keenly aware of her breasts pressing against my chest through her sweater. "I confess I spent most of the third period daydreaming about nipples clamps and handcuffs and your hand fisted in my hair while you fucked my mouth."

My cock is instantly rock-hard and ready to give her everything she wants and more. I lean in, bringing my lips to the perfect pink shell of her ear as I whisper, "Yes, Curious. I will make you sorry for being such a bad girl, and then I will make you come so many times you'll forget your own name."

"Never been fond of my name anyway, sir." She presses a kiss to my cheek that is every bit as sweet as she is.

My sweet, dirty girl, who I truly could not love any more than I do right now, with my heart bursting with gratitude for the second chance we've been given.

I'm riding so high that by the time I finally get her back to the hotel I'm desperate to have her naked and under me. All I want to do is scoop her into my arms, carry her to bed, and make love to her until we're both too tired to move. But she wants pain before her pleasure, and I want her to have everything she wants, everything she needs, everything she's learned to crave because she was made for this, for me.

We were meant to be—it's clear in every touch, from the rough pinch of my fingers on her nipples as I prep them for the clamps to the gentle way I carry her to the bath hours later.

I lay Hailey in the hot water and climb in behind her, guiding her to lie back on my chest as I reach for the soap and lather it between my palms. I start with her arm, massaging her warm skin with slick hands.

"That feels so good," she sighs, only to flinch as I near her wrist. "But maybe not there."

"Tender?" I ask.

"A little."

I lift her arm to the light, noting several faint bluish places beneath the skin. "You might have some bruising from the cuffs. I can go buy some arnica cream when we're done with our bath."

Hailey hums lazily. "Don't worry about it. It's late, and it's not a big deal."

"You don't mind being marked?" I skim soapy fingers across her clavicle before teasing the valley between her breasts.

"Right now, I don't mind anything at all," she says, lifting her chest until her breasts break the surface of the water. Her nipples are hard, making it impossible to keep my hands from sliding down, gliding lightly over those tight tips.

But even that gentle touch makes her wince.

"Tender here, too?" I ask, my cock thickening as a

shudder rocks through her body in response to my soapy fingers circling her areolas.

She nods, her damp hair sliding against my chest. "Yes. But don't stop. Please don't stop."

"Never," I promise as I continue to ever so gently take her there again. I wash every inch of her before letting the water out of the bath, gently parting her thighs, and easing into her from behind.

As I glide in and out with one hand at her swollen breast and the other teasing over her clit, I tell her how much I love her, how much I need her. I tell her how good she feels and how perfect she is and how I will never want anything but her. Finally, as she comes on my cock, the sweet grip of her slickness on my engorged flesh triggering my own release, I groan against her throat, "Mine, Hailey. You're mine. Fuck baby, tell me you're mine."

"Yours," she gasps, fingers threading into mine as we ride out our fourth or fifth orgasm of the night. "I'm yours, Will, all yours, baby, all yours."

And fool that I am, I believe her.

I do not doubt, I do not question, I do not force myself to stay awake, memorizing the way it feels for her to sleep, warm and heavy, on my chest. I slip into unconsciousness moments after Hailey, trusting that we have thousands of more nights like this one to look forward to, trusting that the future is nothing but hearts and flowers and fuzzy handcuffs as far as the eye can see.

CHAPTER 19

I wake in the darkness to the sound of my phone buzzing beside the bed and the pitter-patter of Vancouver drizzle outside our hotel window. I see Bree's name on the screen and fumble for the phone, unease prickling up my spine as I read the time on the hotel clock—4:12 a.m.

Nothing good happens at four in the morning. I know that even before I croak, "Hello, Bree?" and hear my sister sob on the other end of the line.

I sit up fast, sleep-haze vanishing in a cold rush of fear. "Honey? Bree? Are you okay? What's wrong?"

"I need you to p-pick me up at the police station," she says, her voice thick with tears. "I can't d-drive, and I can't stand to call Mom and Dad, I just can't."

Raking a hand through my hair, I swing my legs to the floor, pacing away from the bed as Will sits up, murmuring, "What's wrong?"

I shake my head at him as I ask Bree, "Why, babe? Are you hurt? Were you in an accident?"

"Creedence is a horrible person," she whispers, breaking my heart into tiny, terrified little pieces. "Just like Will and Shane said. I should have listened to them."

"Oh, honey," I say, my throat going tight.

Before I can ask, before I can form the question I hate more than anything I've ever had to ask my sweet little sister, Bree says, "He didn't rape me, but he tried, sissy. And I did a shit job of fighting him and got all messed up. You would have been so disappointed in me. I'm sorry I didn't come to class more often, Hailey, I'm sorry." She breaks off, sobbing so hard I can feel her pain pouring into me over the phone, making me ache to hold her.

"Don't you dare apologize." My voice breaks as I add, "I love you so much, and I'm so glad you're alive. And this is going to be okay, Bree. I'll be there as fast as I can. I'm in Vancouver. I can catch the next plane out, but I doubt I'll be able to get home until nine or ten a.m. at the very earliest. Are you sure you don't want me to call Mom? She won't freak out and threaten to kill anyone like Dad will, and she can be there a lot faster than I can."

"But she told me not to go to his apartment until I knew him better, and I did it anyway," Bree whimpers. "And I can't stand to see her cry, Hailey. I don't want to hurt Mom on top of everything else. Please...I'll wait as long as it takes, just come and get me whenever you can. I'm too scared to go home by myself, and I don't want any of my friends to see me like this."

"All right," I promise, dimly aware of Will on the phone behind me, asking someone about flights to Portland. I'm filled with a rush of gratitude so intense, I have to sink into the chair in the corner to catch my breath.

Thank God for Will, for this good man who never hesitates to help, to care, to do what's right in a world where so many assholes don't hesitate to dole out hurt and pain. By the time I've calmed Bree down the best I can and promised I'll call her as soon as I get to the airport, Will is off the phone and my suitcase is on the bed.

"You're on the next flight out, leaving at six a.m. They only had one ticket, so I'll follow you later today," he says, unzipping the top of the case. "You pack and get dressed, I'll call for a car. If you leave in the next ten minutes, you shouldn't have any trouble clearing security in time."

"Thank you." My hands shake as I toss my phone on the bureau and start toward him. "Thank you so much, babe."

Will meets me halfway, pulling me into his arms for a fiercely sweet hug. "No thanks needed. Let's just get you to Bree, and I'll get to both of you as soon as I can. We're going to make this better, like you said. She's a survivor, and she's got so many people who love her."

I nod against his chest, tightening my arms around him one last time before pulling away. "You're right. She does. I'll be ready to go in ten."

He squeezes my arm gently as he promises, "It's going to be okay."

And I believe him because he's Will, and he's always

had a way of making me believe everything is going to be all right.

I believe all the way to the airport, through security, the flight home, and the trudge through customs. I believe him in the cab to my apartment and as I drive across town to fetch Bree from the police station. I believe right up until the moment I see my little sister sitting on a couch with a black eye and a split lip. Until I see the bruises circling her wrists where a man twice her size held her down while she fought with everything in her to be free.

Until I sit down next to her and take her hand only to realize that the bruises on her wrists aren't much worse than the bruises on mine.

They're almost mirror images, in fact.

Shame floods through me, making my skin feel too small and my throat too tight, I tug the sleeves of my sweater down, but it's too late. Bree squeezes my fingers as she shakes her head. "It isn't the same thing, Hailey. It's okay."

"No, it's not," I whisper, fighting tears as I brush her hair gently from her face, frowning as I take in the purple and red blooming around her swollen eye. "But it's going to be. You're pressing charges?"

Bree nods and clings tighter to my hand. "Yes. He messed with the wrong girl this time."

"I'm so proud of you," I say, wrapping my arm around her slim shoulders.

"You wouldn't have been," Bree says, leaning her head against mine. "I totally choked, Hails. I got scared and forget everything you ever taught me until it was almost too late. I barely made it out of his apartment, and if his neighbor across the hall hadn't been coming home from work..."

She trails off, and I hug her closer in the loaded silence that follows. "I'm always proud of you, and we all choke. When you're ready, we'll just practice harder. And we'll do some creative visualization."

Bree huffs softly. "I always thought those exercises were silly, but you're right. I think it would have helped. If I had imagined myself fighting back before I actually had to do it in real life..." She sniffs then adds in a voice that reminds me of the little girl she was not so long ago, "Can we go home to your place now? I want to stay with you and maybe move in with you because your building has a doorman and I don't want to be a tough girl living in a sketchy apartment anymore."

"Of course. Let's go home, and I'll make bacon pancake breakfast, just the way you like." I kiss her temple as I guide her up and toward the exit, silently promising not to let her out of my sight again until I'm certain I've prepared her properly, the way I should have before.

But I know lack of preparation on my part wasn't the problem.

The problem is that we live in a world where one in four children are sexually assaulted by an adult, where college campuses are breeding grounds for more rapists than honor students, and where, in the most extreme cases, a man feels justified driving a van into a crowd of women, mowing down innocent people because he isn't getting laid as often as he would prefer.

We live in a world where violence against women is trivialized and normalized, and we're taught to think "it's not that bad" when we escape with only a black eye and a handful of bruises, when the rape is merely *attempted* rather than completed.

And for the past three weeks, I've been part of the problem. I've been giving away my power, falling to my knees, practically begging to be treated like an object, or at the very least like something less than fully human.

The word "submissive" means to yield to the established power structure, to humbly accept the status quo. And at this time, in this place, the status quo is seriously in need of an overhaul.

I've always been proud that I teach women to fight back, to assert that they are as worthy of freedom, respect, and bodily integrity as their male counterparts. I've been proud to flip that finger to the status quo, despite being raised to be one of the "good girls."

I'm not just a good girl. I'm also a cancer survivor, a fighter, a scrapper from way back. Years ago, long before I developed curves or understood what a woman was expected to be and survive in this world, I gazed into the dark unknown on the other side of this life and kept my eyes open.

I didn't flinch. I didn't blink.

I stared at the void, and the void stared back, and I knew then that life would never frighten me the way it had before. Once you've stood your ground against the biggest mystery of all, everything else—even the most terrifying creature lurking in the darkest corner on the roughest street—seems smaller in comparison.

But seeing my sister beaten and bruised isn't a small thing.

And knowing I've let down my guard against the disease that created the man who thought it was his right to take what he wanted from her, to treat her like an object to be used for his pleasure and beaten when she didn't meekly submit to that abuse, sickens me to the core.

And I haven't simply stopped fighting; I became part of the problem. Deep down, wasn't that why I hated what I overheard that night on the roof so much? Because I knew it placed Will and I forever on opposite sides of an impassable divide? That a love for dominating women lumped him in with a group of men I found indefensible?

But somehow, in the past six months, when missing my other half became too much to carry, the need to find a way back to Will became more important than my need to stand up for what I believe in. It became more important than what's right. I put getting off ahead of my principles and became someone I'm ashamed of.

As I drive home, my sleeves sliding up to reveal the bruises lacing my wrists, I am ashamed. As I draw Bree a bath—sweater pushed up to my elbows to keep it dry as I test the water—I am ashamed. As I change into leggings and a long-sleeved tee to watch movies with Bree on the couch, I cringe at the evidence of who I am now.

The bruises on my wrists aren't the only marks, the only damage sustained on my way down to rock bottom.

Looking at the nearly healed rope burn on my ankle and the rug burn on my knees, it's all I can do to fight back tears. As I wash my hands, meeting my own shamed, miserable gaze in the mirror, I know what I have to do. No matter how badly it hurts, no matter how much the weak part of me wants to stay on my knees, I have to end this experiment, this terrible mistake.

Before submissive Hailey has a chance to talk me out of my decision, I grab my phone from the kitchen table and type out a quick text to Will—*I've got Bree, and she's going to be okay, but don't call or come over. She needs one-on-one sister time right now. I'll text you as soon as I can. Love you.*—and then shut off my phone.

I do love him. Fiercely. Deeply. Forever.

But that doesn't matter as much as Bree matters, as much as her safety and the safety of the women I love and the girls I teach and the legacy I want to leave behind. When I fade into that final mystery, I want to go with no regrets and no shameful karma dragging at my soul.

So when Bree falls asleep on the couch mid-afternoon, I slip into my room, open up my laptop, and compose the hardest email I've ever written in my life. And then I hit send, curl up in a ball in the center of my bed, and cry without making a sound.

I refuse to wake Bree, to make her worry, or to hurt her a single bit more than I've hurt her already. And this pain will fade. Eventually. And then I will be able to look into the mirror and be proud of the woman in the reflection again.

That's important. Worth sacrificing something for. Everything for...

He feels like everything. Like my heart, ripped out of my body. Going cold on the floor.

CHAPTER 20

The email hits my inbox just as I'm getting back from a run. I'm still soaked with sweat when I pull it up on my phone, certain it's going to be an update from Hailey on her sister and what I can do to help. Maybe she needs me to make a grocery stop or a wine run—Hailey rarely drinks, but I know Bree enjoys a glass of wine now and then, and surely the poor kid could use something to take the edge off after the night she had.

I'm thinking about what else I should bring over to Hailey's—some cookies from the macaroon place on my corner, my old gaming system in case they want to zone out with an alien-killing RPG, or Monopoly for old-fashioned board-game therapy—when I read the first line of the email and realize this isn't what I thought it was.

Record scratching in my head, I go back, reading the first line again, my stomach hardening into a rancid ball as I realize what's happening, what she's doing, how fast all our dreams are burning to the ground.

To: Saunders_Will

From: HaileyRaeRawr

Subject: What we need…

Dear Will,

I'm going to start with "I'm sorry" even though I know it's not enough.

But I am sorry. So sorry.

I thought I could be what you wanted me to be, but I can't.

No matter how much a part of me wants to be the girl kneeling by the door when you get home, that's not who I am.

Or maybe it is.

I don't know…

I'm not sure exactly who I am or what I want anymore, everything's so mixed up in my head, but I do know one thing for sure—I need to fight on the side that protects the innocent and defends the defenseless and helps create a world where men like the monster who hurt Bree understand that women aren't objects or toys or trash. Before I die, I want the world to be a better place than it is now, and that's not going to happen if I spend the rest of my life giving away my power.

Yes, I've loved every second of the games we played. And yes, I understand that consensual power exchange isn't the same thing as what happened to Bree, but it's too close for comfort, Will.

I was holding Bree's hand today, and we had matching bruises. And how can I promise to protect her when I look like a victim myself?

I can't. And I won't. I won't do that to her or to the other people I love.

But I will always love you and treasure you and wish you all the best of everything. You deserve it.

Please don't write back, at least not for a while. I'm weak right now and need time to get strong again.

So sorry,

Hailey

Cursing, it's all I can do not to throw my phone at the brick wall of my building.

But if I throw my phone, I won't be able to text Hailey, and I'm going to text her. I'll respect her need for physical space, but there's no way I can let this stand without responding.

She's got it all wrong. What we do in the bedroom has nothing to do with rape culture or the shitty way women are treated by men who have fucked up notions about what Dominance really means.

Dominance means responsibility and respect, not imposing your will on someone else without their consent. Every game Hailey and I have played, every line we've crossed, every boundary we've blurred, has been agreed upon in advance. She's given her consent and can withdraw that consent at any time with her safe word. I may be the one tying her to the bed, but she's the one who's ultimately in control.

That's the opposite of what happened to Bree, and we're both part of the good fight.

I have to make her see that.

I have to show her that she doesn't have to run or push me away. We don't have to suffer through another year apart, another day apart. We can have our happy ever after and our kinky ever after and still hold our heads high at the annual fundraising banquet for the women's shelter next door to our gym.

I compose my text swiftly, but carefully, pacing back and forth on the sidewalk outside my building, too keyed up to be penned in by four walls.

I explain my thoughts, make my most compelling arguments, and end with an appeal straight from the heart—*I love you, Hailey. More than any lifestyle choice or game or anything else. I think we've both enjoyed our lessons, and I don't see any reason we should have to stop doing something we enjoy, but if it means that much to you, I can be done with it all. Right now. This very fucking second. There is nothing in my life that means as much to me as you do. Your heart is the most precious thing I've ever been entrusted with, baby. If you'll just keep trusting me, I swear I won't let you down. Just keep the lines of communication open, and we'll get through this. Together. All my love, your sexy boyfriend.*

I wait for ten minutes. Twenty.

At the half-hour mark, I force myself to head upstairs to my condo and take a shower. I bring my phone with me into the bathroom so I can listen for the ding of an incoming text, but my cell remains silent—

silent for the rest of the afternoon, silent for the entire next day, silent as I wake on Saturday morning to dark gray skies and the sound of thunder.

Over coffee, I transcribe the text into an email and send it to her that way—pathetically hoping her lack of response is due to some glitch that resulted in my text not being delivered—but within an hour I receive a reply.

To: Saunders_Will

From: HaileyRaeRawr

Subject: I can't

I'm sorry, Will, but I can't do this. I need to stay focused on helping Bree get back on her feet. I can't debate or negotiate with you right now. I'm too confused, and I don't trust myself the way I did before. Our lessons turned my world upside down, and if that isn't proof that I made a mistake, I don't know what is.

I guess I'm not as strong as either of us thought I was.

Good luck at the game tonight, and be careful on your way to the arena. This storm is supposed to get worse before it gets better.

Hailey

"Get worse before it gets better," I murmur aloud as I shut my laptop, forcing myself to give Hailey the space she needs.

I want to write back immediately and tell her that

she is strong, that confusion is a natural part of growth and change, and that I have no doubt she's going to come through to the other side of this and realize there's nothing wrong with the way we love each other, even when that love is expressed with handcuffs and a spanking.

But that would be a lie…at least the last part.

I'm not sure she's going to come through to the other side or that she's going to come back to me or that I will ever get to hold her the way I did that last night in Vancouver. The only thing I'm sure of is that everything is going to get worse before it gets better.

Or maybe just get worse. Period.

Leaving my laptop closed and quiet, I stand and start my day, a day without Hailey in it. A day that will be darker than those that came before, no matter what happens with this damned storm.

CHAPTER 21

WILL

*I*t's a shit night at the end of a shit week, and the last thing I want to do is fight my way through this nightmare storm to play hockey. On my way to the arena, I catch a weather report saying several funnel clouds have been spotted off the coast and naively hope the game might be canceled due to inclement weather.

But the Badgers fans are die-hard ones, and "cancellation" isn't in management's vocabulary.

I arrive in the locker room soaked through from the brief dash from the parking lot and find the rest of the team in similar spirits. The fact that we're playing one of the lowest ranked teams in the league—a new expansion team out of Kansas City with a meh fan base and a meh reputation and a meh game—doesn't help improve morale. There's no rivalry to get us fired up, no history, and not much on the line for the Badgers.

We know we're going to beat these guys, it's just a matter of by how many goals.

We're cocky, yes, but we have reason to be, and I have no reason to assume this game is even going to distract me from my miserable life for a few hours.

We hit the ice a few minutes after seven o'clock, accompanied by a roar from our fans and a crash of thunder, and that's about as exciting as things get for the next hour and a half.

First period, we score three easy goals right in a row, so quickly the fans start to seem a little let down by the lack of drama. But by the time Nowicki slams goal four into the opposing team's net, our fans are chanting the Kansas City goalie's name in a jeering way that leaves the poor bastard so red in the face he looks like a blister about to pop.

The second period is more of the same, until the score is six-zero and we start to feel bad for being so awesome. But then again, we're not actually playing all that well.

Comparison...it's the thief of joy.

If I'd never had these past few weeks with Hailey, for example, I wouldn't be on the verge of ripping my own hands off to keep from texting her again. I would still be missing her and wishing we could have worked things out, but I wouldn't know how perfectly with fit together as Dominant and submissive. I wouldn't know beyond a shadow of a doubt that we were meant to be, perfectly matched in every way, crafted by some higher power to fit together the way my custom molded skate boot cradles my wedge-shaped foot.

She is my woman, and I'm her man.

I will never belong to anyone the way I belong to Hailey, and the thought of her moving on without me, of her sharing her body and her heart—that beautiful, brave heart that no man could ever treasure the way I do—makes me physically fucking ill. Even as I play as hard as I can be expected to play against such subpar opponents, my stomach is roiling, threatening to bring up my chicken and rice for a second showing on national television.

And that's before I see a Kansas City defenseman taking a run at Nowicki as he heads to the bench. My teammate's back is turned, and he has no idea that two-hundred and thirty pounds of sore loser is about to slam him into the boards. I take off fast, moving first and thinking somewhere between center ice and the bench that I should have probably eaten more protein. I'm one hundred and eighty-five pounds on a good week, when I haven't been fucking when I should be carbo-loading. Back when Hailey and I were a couple, I was so grounded in her, in us, that I never forgot to take care of myself. But these past few days without her, I've slipped.

I haven't slept, I've barely eaten, I'm low on energy, and when I try to slip between Nowicki and the bastard with his stick clutched in both hands, ready to cross-check my friend, I'm two seconds too late.

I don't make it in time. I watch in slow motion as Nowicki takes the stick hard to the shoulder and goes tumbling head first into the bench, no chance to break the fall he never saw coming.

There's no time for me to slow down, either.

Bright arena lights reflect off of something in motion, but before my mind can process what it is, the blade of Nowicki's skate is already slicing across my throat.

Mostly I feel pressure sharp in soft skin. Then heat. More heat. Flowing under my shoulder pads making sweat-slick skin even stickier. The pain hits a good five seconds later, at the same time our trainer jumps over the boards with a towel he presses urgently to my throat.

I'm confused for a moment, and then I realize that I'm bleeding. Badly. Not long after, before I can decide whether to crawl over the boards to the bench or to sit down where I am on the ice, I start to feel cold. Really cold. And dizzy, despite the fact that I'm not bothered by blood.

I'm a gallon donor. And I grew up playing pond hockey. Bloody noses and split lips were a daily occurrence. Also, I'm not a fucking wimp; I'm a grown man who plays hockey for a living. I do not get weak in the knees because I have an owie.

But that's what happens. My knees go weak, the lights of the arena blur and spin above me as I go down hard, the trainer following me down with his towel. It's wet now and heavy. Hot and heavy. Something has really fucked up that towel.

Something that smells like metal and meat.

And me.

It's blood. A lot of blood.

Shit.

That's my last upright thought—*shit*. And then I'm flat on the ice in a puddle of my own blood. As the world goes dark, I wonder if I'm going to be the second ever on-ice death in the NHL, and I hope that Hailey isn't watching. No one should have to watch the person they love die on national television.

She still loves me, even if we didn't work out. I know that much, and it's enough to give me some cold comfort as I go black.

CHAPTER 22

HAILEY

*I*t happens so fast that by the time I realize Will's bleeding, he's going down, a bright red towel pressed to his neck. But it's not the towel that's red. It's his blood, soaking the fibers then spreading out on the ice, turning the choppy, mid-game surface crimson.

I stand up fast, bolting up from the couch where Bree and I have been vegging all evening only to freeze as the announcer's voice cuts in, muting the hushed murmurs of concern filling the sold-out arena. "Medics are on the ice, players standing back to give them access. Looks like this is the most serious injury we've seen this season, Jim."

The second commentator responds, "That's the worst injury I've seen in my fifteen years broadcasting pro hockey, Dan. Will Saunders taking what appears to be a skate *deep* to the throat. Yikes." He sucks in a breath through his teeth, a sound that makes my already tight jaw clench even tighter. "Here's hoping they can get him help ASAP. We'll keep you updated as soon as we have more information, folks, but certainly all the fans out in Badgerland are sending hopes and prayers to Will and his family tonight, wishing him a swift recovery."

The station goes to commercial just as two medics are loading Will onto a stretcher, with a jarring cut to a close up of a garishly thick burger oozing with melted cheese. My hand flies to my mouth, covering my lips as the stir-fry I had for dinner rises in my throat.

"Oh my God," Bree murmurs, muting the television then tossing the remote on the couch and rising to stand beside me. "Hailey, it's going to be okay. He's going to be okay. He's Will. He's so strong, you know that."

I shake my head, my hand still clamped over my mouth, my thoughts racing too fast to pick any words out of the swirling chaos in my head.

All I can seem to think about is skin—how thin it is. How delicate. How this fragile barrier is all that stands between whole and broken, between life and death.

Death...

He could die. *Will* could die.

If he loses enough blood, if the medics can't get it stopped in time, if his heart can't take the stress.

His heart...

His precious, perfect, irreplaceable heart...

He might never know how much it means to me, how much *he* means to me. He might be leaving me tonight, and he's going to go out thinking I don't care, at least not enough, and from this minute to my last minute I will regret that more than words can express.

I still have no words, but finally my thoughts jump-start my body into action.

I have to go to him.

Now.

Right fucking now.

I bolt for the door, grabbing my phone from the kitchen table as I pass and shoving it into my purse as I jam my feet into my tennis shoes, pushing hard to fit my fluffy bedtime socks inside. There isn't time to change my socks or my clothes, and I couldn't care less if everyone at the arena sees me in my pajamas.

There isn't a second to waste. Not one single second.

I'm dimly aware of Bree following me across the room, of her hands pulling my hair from under my collar as I shrug on my coat and her voice murmuring something about driving safe, but it's all a blur.

The world is melting and nothing is in focus except the fear, sharp and gleaming.

I may never see the man I love again.

Never. Again.

Those two words make everything that's happened the past few days seem so small and stupid, and the Hailey who thought she could shut off the parts of her heart that weren't fitting neatly into the approved boxes seem pitiably naïve. Some things are bigger than boxes and rules. Things like the kind of primal, soul-deep, bone-deep love I feel for Will.

It's bigger than the rules. Bigger than a bruise on my

wrist or the panic that said losing control in the bedroom meant I was losing control of my life.

Will and I are stronger than fear, and he's right—what happened to Bree has nothing to do with us. The way we choose to love each other has nothing to do with the way a man chose to hate my sister. The bruises on her wrist might mirror the bruises on mine, but they're no more alike than art hanging in a museum and the crude scrawl of gang graffiti under a crumbling bridge.

Now that the fear has cut all the bullshit away and left me standing with my heart throbbing fitfully in my hands and a voice deep inside crying out Will's name, it's so clear. It's so clear that it's all I can hear, all I can see.

I don't remember riding the elevator down to the garage or starting the car or pulling up the ramp toward the exit. My body is on autopilot, and my soul already miles away with Will, begging him to fight, to hold on, to wait until I get there and somehow I will make this better. I will find a way.

I will open my veins, I will hold his delicate skin together with my bare hands, I will fight off Death using every dirty trick in the book. I will hit below the belt, jab my keys into Death's throat, scratch out his eyes, whatever it takes to keep Will here with me where he belongs.

I'm so focused, so consumed by the need to get across town as quickly as humanly possible, that it takes a long moment for me to realize the high-pitched hum filling the car isn't coming from inside my own head. By the time I acknowledge that my phone is ringing, the call has already clicked over to voicemail.

At the next red light, I tug it out of my purse as a text message from Laura, the Badger's PR manager and the team captain's wife, pops through—*They're taking Will to the Good Samaritan ER on 22nd Street. I don't know if you were watching the game, but he was injured pretty badly and is on his way to get sewn up. Don't worry, I'm sure he's going to be fine, but I thought you should know.*

Hands shaking, I type back a quick—*Thank you. On my way there now*—and toss the phone back into my purse as the light turns green.

Fifteen minutes later, I've parked outside the ER and run inside only to be told that Will is already in surgery. I scan the waiting room, but I don't recognize anyone from the team. Everyone else must still be at the game. The show goes on. The game has rules that must be followed, even when one of the players might be dying.

It's macabre. Twisted. Wrong.

The game should have stopped. The world should have stopped, its rotation put on pause until we know for sure that Will is going to be all right.

But it doesn't stop and an hour later familiar faces begin to trickle into the ER—Brendan and a very pregnant Laura first, followed quickly by Petrov, Shane, Cruise and his sweet wife Libby, and a couple of new players I don't recognize. Shane makes the introductions, but I forget the names as soon as I hear them.

I'm in shock, so numbed by fear that I don't realize how hot the coffee cup Laura presses into my hands is until I scald my tongue on my first sip.

The next hour passes slower than any in memory, each minute dragging miserably into the next until the doctor finally pushes through the double doors and strides toward our corner of the waiting room, wiping his hands on a paper towel as he moves. "Will is out of surgery, and his vitals are good, but he lost a lot of blood. We're going to be monitoring him in the recovery room for the next several hours, and he'll need his rest after. I recommend you all go home and get some rest, too, and check back in the morning. It's going to be a while before he's ready for visitors."

After a brief discussion in which Laura promises to keep everyone updated on Will's condition, the rest of the team says their good nights and heads for the door.

Soon Shane and I are the only people left in our corner. We sit in silence for a long time, watching the seemingly endless stream of people flowing into the ER. The storm is certainly claiming its share of victims. Despite the abundance of wet stuff that falls on Rose City each year, the people of Portland aren't great on the road in a normal rain, let alone a monster storm like this one.

The thought's barely through my head when thunder booms loud enough to vibrate the wall behind me.

I shiver, pulling my coat tighter around me as I say, "It feels like the world's trying to end, doesn't it?"

"Nah, the sky's just having a fit," Shane says. "The world is going to be okay. And so is Will. He's tough, Hailey. It's going to take more than a skate in the neck and a little blood loss to take him down."

I nod, but the ache in my chest doesn't subside. "I just wish I could see him. Even if he's asleep, if I could just see his face…"

"Soon. And I'll stay with you until you can go back," Shane says, making me smile.

"You're sweet. Thank you."

He shakes his head. "No, I'm not sweet. I suck. I heard what happened to Bree. I should have tried harder to get through to her about Creedence. I should have worried more about keeping her safe than whether she thought I had a silly crush. If I had…"

I lay a hand on his strong arm, giving it a gentle squeeze. "No way. That isn't your fault. Not even a little bit."

Shane sniffs. "Yeah, well, it feels like it's my fault."

"I know what you mean," I say softly. "It felt like my fault, too, but it's not. The only one to blame is the man who lifted his hands to her."

It's true. No one else is to blame. Not Shane, not me, not Will, and not the consensual things we did in private out of love for each other. I can't wait to tell him that, to see his face, to kiss his forehead and promise that I'll never let myself get so confused again. Or at the very least that I'll talk things through with him and not just push him away.

I just hope he'll still want to hear that from me.

I hope he hasn't given up on me. On us.

Sometime during the night, I must have nodded off because I wake with a start, jerking my head from Shane's shoulder, cheeks heating as I see the small spot of drool I've left on his jean jacket. "I'm so sorry."

He glances down at the saliva spot with a shrug. "No worries. But I think they're ready for us." He motions toward the double doors leading into the bowels of the hospital, where a dark-haired nurse is waiting expectantly.

I stand so fast, the world spins, and I'm grateful for the hand Shane places on my back when I stumble before finding my footing.

"No rush, honey," the nurse says with a tired smile. "He's not going anywhere, though he sure would like to be. We may have to strap that one to the bed to convince him to stay put long enough to heal."

I thread my fingers together, squeezing them into a fist. "Oh good. I mean, not good, but it's good to hear that he's feeling okay."

"He insisted he was ready to be discharged," she says with a laugh as she leads the way down the long hall and through another set of doors to an elevator. "But we convinced him to stay with us a little longer. He's in a private room on the third floor, but I know the shortcut."

Heart beating faster, I step into the elevator between the nurse and Shane. I'm so close. In just a few more minutes, I'll be able to see Will's face, look into his eyes, and know that he's really okay. To know if *we're* okay.

Out of the elevator and down another hall and my pulse is racing in my throat and my heart is there, too, lodged fast. And then I follow the nurse through the door and see Will, propped up in bed, pale and with a bandage wrapped around his throat, but whole and okay and mine.

Still mine.

The second our gazes connect, and relief and love soften his features, I know it's not too late. Tears stinging into my eyes, I cross the room and take his hand, squeezing tight. "Hey there. Good to see you in one piece."

Will's lips curve as he grips my hand just as tightly. "Good to see you, too," he says, his voice soft and rough, but still strong, still Will's. "And I love you. I promised myself that would be the first thing I'd say if I got to see you again."

I press my lips together, fighting back tears. "I love you, too. I'm so glad you're okay. And I'm so sorry I've been a confused pain in the ass."

"You are never a pain in the ass. You're my favorite person," Will says, gaze shifting to focus over my shoulder. "Thanks for staying with her last night."

"My pleasure," Shane says from behind me, clearing his throat. "But now that you're awake I'm going to go. Don't want to be a third wheel. Just wanted you to know we're all here for you, the whole team, anything you need while you're laid up, just let us know."

"Thanks, man, I appreciate it," Will says as I turn and lift a hand to Shane, echoing my thanks with a grateful smile.

And then he's gone, and Will and I are alone in the small hospital room, where the morning sky is just beginning to peek through the clouds outside the window, and I feel hopeful again. And grateful. But also a little ashamed of myself for needing something like this to pull my head out of my ass.

"I'm sorry," I say, perching carefully on the edge of the bed. "It shouldn't have taken thinking you were going to die for me to realize I couldn't live without you."

Will holds my gaze as he shakes his head. "Don't apologize. I get it, baby. And I don't blame you. We've been exploring some emotionally intense new territory, and then your sister was attacked. It's okay that you were confused about how to reconcile everything you were feeling. Just promise me, the next time something like this happens, you won't shut me out."

"No more shutting you out or pushing you away," I promise before adding in a stern voice, "But nothing like this is allowed to happen for a long, long time. No more attacks on people I love, not from assholes or skates or anything else."

His lips quirk on one side. "Amen, woman. I could stand for this to be the last injury I see for a while. I've decided that I really prefer having my head attached to my body."

I cup his cheek gently in my hand. "I prefer that, too. And I prefer you to be you. You don't have to give up anything for me. You were right, the way we enjoy loving each other has nothing to do with the things that are wrong with the world."

"Are you sure?" His brow furrows as he rests his hand on my waist, even that simple touch enough to make me feel safe, loved, and like I'm exactly where I'm supposed to be. "Because I meant every word I sent in that email this morning, Hailey. There is nothing in the world as important to me as you are. As long as you're mine, I could give up being part of the scene forever and not regret it for a single fucking second. I swear it."

"I know you mean that," I assure him, "but I mean this, too. I've been thinking all night…" I pause, looking for the perfect words to express the truth that's so clear to me now. "I thought I had to deny a part of myself to be strong for my sister and my students and all the women I care about. But the bravest choice I can make is to be myself, to accept every part of myself as worthy of expression, even the parts that might be hard for me to reconcile with the rest of my life." I gaze into his kind eyes, wondering how I ever doubted that we could make this work, that we can make anything work as long as we love each other the way we do. "I treasured every second of our lessons, and I love the way I feel when we're together that way. I don't want either of us to give up something that feels so right if we don't absolutely have to. And I don't think we do."

His fingers curl lightly into my hip as he nods. "Then we'll take it one day at a time and keep the lines of communication open. And whatever path we choose, as long as we choose it together, I'm going to be the happiest man in the world, sweetheart. I promise you."

"So does that mean you still want to be a couple again?" I ask, hope thinning my voice. "Because I would really love to tell Bree that she can have my safe, doorman-protected apartment and move back in with this man I love beyond all decency or reason."

"Decency and reason are overrated, and hell yes, you're moving back in." A wide grin breaks across his face only to end in a wince. "Shit, it hurts to smile that hard."

"Then don't smile that hard," I say, rising from the bed. "I should go and let you get some rest. Do you need me to bring you anything? Some pajamas from home or DVDs or books? Something to keep you distracted until they spring you from this joint?"

"Nope," he says, without missing a beat. "I've got everything I need right here, and I don't need rest. Now get your ass into this bed with me and let me hold you."

"But I don't want to hurt you," I say, hesitating, though there's nothing I want more than to wrap my arms around Will and never let go.

"I've been stitched up good and tight," he says, waving me up. "I'm not going to break that easily. Now, woman. That's an order."

"Well, in that case…" I wink as I toe off my tennis shoes and crawl carefully into bed beside him, curling an arm around his waist as I rest my head lightly on his chest. He sighs in response, a sound of gratitude and relief that echoes the emotion swelling inside me.

"You and me," I promise, laying my hand over his heart. "From here on out."

"Until death do us part," he says, making me smile as he adds, "And I fully intend to ask you to marry me again before the season is out, so prepare yourself. I'm tired of waiting to see my ring on your finger."

"Or maybe I'll ask you first," I whisper, snuggling closer.

He runs a gentle hand over my hair. "I'll say yes. I'm a sure thing, baby."

"One of the many things I love about you."

"Ditto, Curious." His breathing grows deeper, more rhythmic and within a few minutes I can tell that he's asleep. After a few more moments, I close my eyes and slip away after him, secure in the knowledge that he'll be there when I wake up, today and the next day and for all the tomorrows thereafter.

CHAPTER 23

BREE

Eight months later...

My sister has always been my hero. Long before she beat cancer or graduated valedictorian or made the Thirty Under Thirty Businesswomen in Portland to Watch list, Hailey was my kick-ass sissy and very best friend.

And Will is the big brother I never had, a true knight in shining armor.

Or knight in shining black leather, I guess...since he and Hailey are living kinkily ever after, but I've done my best to put what little I know about my sister's sex life out of my mind. As soon as it was clear that she and Will were back on the road to forever, I did a Jedi mind wipe on myself.

It worked. Mostly...

Though sometimes, when Hailey shows up for a Saturday morning sister date with an especially goofy smile on her face, I do wonder what naughtiness put the spring in her step. I also wonder if I'm ever going to find someone to put a spring in mine, but that kind of worry isn't on the agenda for today.

Today isn't for mourning the state of my tragically ancient hymen; today is for celebrating the awesome and inspiring power of true love. The sun is shining, Oregon is covered in spring green and June flowers, and my sister is getting married on the rooftop of a hotel in McMinnville, Oregon, with vineyards blanketing the surrounding hills and UFO enthusiasts cheering from the streets below.

The UFO enthusiasts weren't a planned part of the celebration—Hailey somehow managed to book her wedding on the same weekend that McMinnville is flooded with people who believe in little green men and green beer and how much fun it is to blend their appreciation for the two during a week-long festival—but I think they add flair and fun.

My mother, however, is not amused.

"What is that on that man's head?" Mom fusses, her blond brow furrowing as she leans over the railing to peer at the street below.

I glance over my shoulder. "Antennae maybe?"

"Do aliens have antennae? Are they like insects? And why is that woman's baby painted blue, honey? She's green, and the baby is blue."

"I'm guessing the father must be blue," I offer dryly. "Or maybe the grandmother or grandfather, but I'm not an expert in alien genetics, so don't quote me."

Mom shifts her narrow gaze my way. "Very funny, Sabrina."

"Just trying to lighten the mood, Mother. It's all in good fun, and Will and Hailey don't seem to mind sharing their special day with people in alien costumes."

"But what if we can't hear the vows?" Mom fluffs her bob with one ring-laden hand as she tsks. "And why are those men dressed like hammers? That makes absolutely no sense."

"Hammerhead alien? Like a hammerhead shark?" I glance back down at the street where the men dressed as hammers are cavorting down the parade route behind a group of cackling witches. "Or it could have something to do with beer. Don't they have a hammerhead ale or something?"

"I have no idea, but I could go for a drink. A strong one," Mom says, making me laugh as I kiss her forehead.

"Then I'll go fetch you one, sweet mama. Don't worry. It's all going to be perfect. You just wait and see."

I cross the roof to the bar on the other side, where a number of the groomsmen are already crowded around a table nursing a pint as they wait for the festivities to begin. I sidle up to the bar beside a familiar pair of broad shoulders and nudge Shane Wallace's elbow with mine. "You ready for this, best man?"

He shakes his head as he shifts my way. "As ready as I'll ever be."

I grin. "Nervous?"

"A little," he admits, rolling his bright blue eyes. "Mostly about the reception toast. As soon as that's over, I'll be golden. I'm not a fan of public speaking."

"Just imagine everyone naked," I offer. "That's what I'm going to do during my speech. It helps."

His lips curve on one side as he clears his throat. "I think I'll pass on that."

"Why?" I tease. "Most of the people here would probably look okay naked. Even my mom's a babe for fifty-two."

Shane's face wrinkles in an expression of horror so intense I can't help but laugh.

"You're evil," he says, nudging me in the ribs with his elbow. "I'm a gentleman, Sabrina. I don't imagine ladies naked, especially ladies old enough to be my mother. Besides, I have my own coping strategy, thank you very much."

"And what's that?" I ask, still giggling.

"Reminding myself that I'm in the home stretch around here. This is my last season with the Badgers. So if I screw up and make a fool of myself, they can only make my life miserable in the locker room for so long."

My smile falls away so fast I flinch like I've dropped something. "Wait. What? Why? You aren't quitting hockey, are you? You love hockey."

Shane's dark blond brows draw together. "No, I'm not quitting. I was transferred to Kansas City. I thought you knew. Hailey asked if she could invite you to my goodbye BBQ in June, and I said yes..."

"No, she hasn't asked me. At least not yet. But she's been busy with the wedding, so..." I shake my head numbly, feeling strangely abandoned. Shane and I have been hanging out a lot more in the past few months. I thought we'd become good friends, but apparently I was wrong.

Why didn't he tell me himself?

And why do I suddenly want to dive into his arms, hug him so tight he can't breathe, and beg him not to go?

"Brendan's retiring to go coach the new expansion team, and I'm going with him," he continues. "I'm actually looking forward to it. I'll always love Portland, but I'm ready to move on, try something new."

"Yeah, I mean...that's great," I say, feigning interest in scraping a bit of stray pink polish from next to my thumbnail. "I hope it's awesome."

He laugh-grunts. "Why don't I believe you?"

I look up sharply. "No, I do. I just wish you'd told me yourself."

"I just did," he says, holding my gaze with an intensity that makes me feel too warm despite the cool May evening.

"You know what I mean," I murmur, my pulse beating faster.

"No, I'm not sure I do, Bree. I don't think it would have changed anything, do you?"

My mouth opens, closes, opens again, but no words come out. Shane and I have danced around this subject more than once, but he's never gotten this close to flat out saying that he wants more than friendship. And I've never gotten this close to confessing that it's impossible for me to be more than his beer and antique-hunting buddy.

Even though I want to.

Even though I have naughty dreams about sexy Shane Wallace more often than I would like to admit.

Even though he's not only drop dead gorgeous—with soulful sky blue eyes, boy-band perfect tousled blond hair, and a smile that makes my belly flip in strange but lovely ways—he's also tons of fun, adorably goofy, and unfailingly kind.

He would be the perfect Number One if I were capable of making that leap. If I weren't a weirdo with a medical condition crazy enough to ensure I'll probably spend the rest of my life alone.

"Blah," I finally blurt out, because words have failed me.

"Blah?" Shane arches a teasing brow.

"Yes, blah." I flip my bangs from my forehead with a nervous flick of my fingers before I lift a hand to the bartender. "A white wine please, sir. A big, nerve-soothing one. For the mother of the bride."

"Is she having wedding day jitters?" Shane asks, gracefully changing the subject.

"No, I think she has an alien phobia." I lean back against the bar, glancing across the roof to where my mother is still shaking her head and clucking at the UFO parade streaming by below. "Or maybe just a weirdness phobia. Mom likes to color inside the lines."

"It must have been hard for her. Raising a weirdo like you."

Grin curving my lips, I bonk Shane's shoulder with mine. "I am not a weirdo."

"Weird," Shane insists.

"Like you're one to talk. Last time I checked you were still collecting creepy salt and pepper shakers."

"Not creepy. Unique." He pauses, lifting a hand to adjust the flower crown that's been slipping down into my eyes all afternoon. "I have a deep appreciation for unique things. And unique people."

My lips part and electricity prickles sweetly across my skin, promising that this could be the night, that Shane could be the one, that things could be different this time if I'm careful and honest.

But how to be honest about something like my crazy something?

Shane says he likes unique things, but I doubt that applies to the unique insanity of my whacked out immune system. My body turned traitor to love.

Or sex, anyway...

And what man wants love without sex?

Certainly not Shane. He may be a sweetheart, but he also oozes sex. He sizzles with it, exudes an "I'd love to pounce" vibe that makes me anxious when we're alone. It's one of the reasons I prefer to hang out with him in public places, with other friends. I'm afraid that I'll do something, say something, confess something I shouldn't.

I'm allergic to semen, Shane. It makes my entire body break out in hives. Sexy, huh? I can imagine myself saying it now. Can imagine the expression on his face as he realizes I'm definitely not his kind of unique. Not any guy's kind of unique.

Thankfully, before I'm forced to find something to say, I'm saved by the bartender plunking a glass of wine next to my arm. "Thanks." I grip the thin stem like a life-line as I glance back up at Shane. "Good luck. I'm sure your speech will be great. I'll be rooting for you."

"Ditto, doc," he says.

"It's going to be a long time before I'm a doc," I remind him. "If I ever get there."

"You'll get there," he says without a trace of doubt. "I believe in you, Sabrina Marks. And I'll miss you. Take care of your self, okay?"

"Okay," I echo as my heart does a somersault behind my ribs and my throat squeezes tight. Why, oh why, does he have to be like this? So wonderful? So kind? So absolutely irresistible in every way?

The questions linger as I proceed to get my mother gently drunk, ensuring that by wedding go-time she's sufficiently relaxed not to care that someone is blasting the theme song from *The X-Files* so loud it's competing with the wedding march as Hailey glides down the aisle. But it's hard to be stressed out when in the presence of this kind of love. Hailey and Will are shining, glowing, sparkling with love, the pair of them so perfectly in sync in their adoration that the gathered friends and family spend most of the ceremony sighing with sappy happiness.

The reception is just as lovely, with a delicious meal, inspiring toasts—Shane's is as perfect as I expected it to be—and Will and Hailey spinning around the floor for their first dance like they were made to move together, to be two halves of one whole. To be forever.

Forever...

I want that.

But I would be happy with much less—with a summer love or a summer fling. Or maybe just a really sexy June, during which I might finally be able to ditch the V card that's weighing me down, making every obstacle to finding Mr. Right seem even more insurmountable.

Usually I know better than to hope for such things. But whether it's the romance in the air or the moonlight on my skin or that third glass of wine I probably shouldn't have sipped quite so fast, by the time Shane asks me to dance I'm starting to wonder if I've been too hasty.

Too close-minded.

Too eager to shut things down when I should be lighting them up.

As Shane pulls me into his arms, one big hand flat on the small of my back and the other curled around mine, I let myself sway closer than I would have before. I pull the spicy-sweet smell of his cologne deep into my lungs and relish the way his scent makes me ache in places someone who's "just a friend" shouldn't.

Though really, it's his fault for having such strong hands, such pretty muscles, and such a sexy neck. How have I never noticed what a delicious neck this man has? I tilt my head, drifting closer to Shane as one slow song ends and another begins, bringing my nose closer to his smooth skin as I draw in another breath.

"Bree?" His voice is a deep rumble that makes me want to rest my ear on his chest and let the reverberations fill me up like a seashell.

"Yes, Shane," I murmur, starting to feel a little drunk on his scent.

"Are you sniffing me?"

I giggle, clearly tipsier than I thought if he's caught me so easily. "Yes. Sorry. Your cologne is yummy. It reminds me of Christmas, but not in the bad way."

"What could possibly be bad about Christmas?"

"Well, last Christmas, my parents told us they were divorcing, so that sucked," I say, my spontaneous over-share confirming my tipsy suspicions. I should retreat to my room until I recover mouth control, but instead I say, "But I meant the best parts of Christmas. Cider with an extra cinnamon stick and fresh cut pine trees and big fluffy socks warm right out of the drier."

Shane makes a dubious sound, but when I look up at him, he's smiling. "Thank you, but it sounds like I need to find something a little less seasonal for summertime."

"No." I scowl. "I like it. No changing. You're already moving away. That's enough changing."

Shane purses his lips as he nods. "True. I am."

"You're leaving in June?"

"Beginning of July, right after the fourth," he says, his words fanning the hopeful fire smoldering in my chest.

It's crazy. I shouldn't even consider it. I shouldn't even consider considering it.

"So we still have time to make it to the west side for another batch of dirty fries," he says, the word 'dirty' on his full lips making me break out in a fine layer of sweat between my breasts. It's a cool night, and my pink flapper-style bridesmaid's dress is anything but heavy, but I'm clearly losing my mind.

And my self-control.

And my sense of self-preservation.

This isn't just crazy, it's dangerous. But there's something about this night, this man, and Shane's voice as he asks, "You all right, doc?"

I shake my head and lift my chin, bringing my lips closer to his. And then, before I know what my crazy mouth is going to do next, I'm kissing him, pressing onto tiptoe, wrapping my arms around his neck, and going for it with everything in me. For his part, Shane doesn't miss a beat. One moment, there's enough room between us for the Holy Spirit, the next, he's pulled me so close my breasts are flattened against his powerful chest, and our hearts are pounding in time and tingles are sweeping through me from head to toe and back again until I'm dizzy.

Spinning.

Flying with my feet still on the ground.

It is by far the best kiss of my entire life, so hot and intense and all-consuming that I know I have to go for it. Make the leap. Take my stand. Take inspiration from the UFO festival still rocking hard below and make one large step for womankind and ask Shane if he might consider planting his flag in my moon dust.

I pull back, letting the words emerge in a rush, "I really like you so much Shane, and you're so crazy sexy, and I'm all about your body, but I'm allergic to semen. The slightest exposure literally makes my throat swell shut, my eyes go red, and my nose stream snot like that's my job."

Shane's eyes go so wide I'm pretty sure I can see part

of his brain peeking out beneath his lashes, but I'm already in too far to turn back now.

"So if you're up for tackling some crazy shit like that and all the careful containment that would have to go on to make sure I don't die after we bang"—I step out of his arms and back toward the door to the stairs—"then shoot me a text tomorrow, and we can discuss details for a Friends with Benefits situation before you leave. Okay? See ya, great kiss, sleep well, bye." I bolt for the stairs like I'm being chased by zombies—the fast-moving kind, not shuffly, retro zombs—ignoring Shane's call for me to wait until I get halfway down the first set of stairs and realize there's something important I forgot to share.

I sprint back up, opening the door just as Shane is reaching for the handle, and pant into his shocked face, "Also, I'm a virgin, and you would be my first all the way in the va-jay-jay, so take that into consideration, too. Bye, I'm leaving, don't follow me, I have to go lock myself in my room and scream into my pillow because I can't believe I just said all those things to you out loud. The end."

I vanish like a little green alien spotted by the Men in Black, and soon I'm back in my room, hiding under the covers, madly texting the details of my most recent insanity to Stephanie, my friend who teaches yoga to the Badgers on Saturday mornings, and my only friend other than Hailey who knows Shane personally, when another text pops up on my screen.

It's from Shane…

I don't need to think about it. I'm in.

Oh God.

Oh my God.

Oh sweet baby Jesus kidnapped from the manger by an unidentified flying object.

He's in.

And I'm about to have a June I'll never, ever, EVER forget.

Shane and Bree's story continues in
PUCK BUDDIES out Fall 2018.

Keep reading for a sneak peek!

Subscribe to Lili's newsletter and never
miss a sale or new release:
https://www.subscribepage.com/z5x3t4

TELL LILI YOUR FAVORITE PART

I love reading your thoughts about the books and your review matters. Reviews help readers find new-to-them authors to enjoy. So if you could take a moment to leave a review letting me know your favorite part of the story —nothing fancy required, even a sentence or two would be wonderful—I would be deeply grateful.

Thank you and happy reading!

Puck Buddies is out Fall 2018!

Bree Marks is my best friend... My secret crush...

And—wait for it—cursed with a deadly allergy to erecto-plasm. As in she'll seriously swell up and die if seminal fluid even touches her. Which means finding the perfect guy to punch her V card is *literally* a matter of life and death.

She wants a no-strings summer fling, but she needs someone she can trust.

A puck buddy who isn't going to get overly emotional. Someone who's as savvy in the sack as he is on the ice.

That's where I come in.

It's a simple request, really—and one I would be happy to honor.

If it weren't for the whole life-and-death thing.

If I hadn't just been traded to a team thousands of miles away from this girl who makes me think not all relationships are a losing game.

If I wasn't already crazy in love with her.

PUCK BUDDIES is a sexy, standalone romantic comedy from USA Today bestseller Lili Valente.

ABOUT THE AUTHOR

USA Today Bestselling author Lili Valente has slept under the stars in Greece, eaten dinner at midnight with French men who couldn't be trusted to keep their mouths on their food, and walked alone through Munich's red light district after dark and lived to tell the tale.

Find Lili on the web at
www.lilivalente.com

The V Card -co-written with Lauren Blakely

a USA Today Bestseller

Falling for the Boss -co-written
with Sylvia Pierce

Master Me Series
Snowbound with the Billionaire
Snowed in with the Boss
Masquerade with the Master

To the Bone Series
A Love so Dangerous
A Love so Deadly
A Love so Deep

Under His Command Series
Controlling Her Pleasure (Free!)
Commanding Her Trust
Claiming Her Heart

Bought by the Billionaire Series
Dark Domination (Free!)
Deep Domination
Desperate Domination
Divine Domination

Kidnapped by the Billionaire Series

Dirty Twisted Love (Free!)

Filthy Wicked Love

Crazy Beautiful Love

One More Shameless Night

Bedding the Bad Boy Series

The Bad Boy's Temptation (Free!)

The Bad Boy's Seduction

The Bad Boy's Redemption